Obsidian Alcatraz

Obsidian Alcatraz

An Evalyce Novella

J. Aislynn D' Merricksson

Published 2016 by Creativia

Book design by Creativia (www.creativia.org)

Cover art by http://www.thecovercollection.com/

Visit Port Jericho and the Rookery!

www.aislynndmerricksson.com

Visit our Facebook page!

www.facebook.com/Evalyce

This book is dedicated those who are my life-blood
and strong, loving support:
To Brother Wildfire and Mercurius Greyeyes, my deepest
inspirations.
To Jonas Merricksson, twice lucky one, my callowayla.
To Beth Finley, who inspired me to open the door to De Sikkari.
To Michael Calabrase, Goshen, my soul-mate and nemesis.
To Chris and Brandi Gore, anamcara and truest of friends.

To John and Sam Owens, my steady and strong support.

To Anish and Tania, who helped make this possible!
To my family of heart and soul,
To my blood-family and
To my bond-family-
There are far too many of you to name here! I love you all the
same, each and every one.

In loving memory of Nina Clark
who taught me my own Dance
and fostered in me a love of learning.
May the One who is All And Nothing
forever guide your steps.
Nasmala!

Skycity of Port Jericho, 10000 ft above the Aeryth Ocean, Year of the Jade Bull, 2114 CE

The scent of blood hung heavy in the air. Cadi sighed and pulled out her pouch of gravening dust. Pouring a bit into her hand, she blew a breath out and the sparkling dust adhered to the surface of the door before her, revealing a tangled criss-cross of fingerprints. Once visible, the fingerprints were easy collect onto slender glass slides. It would be up to Jupiter, the Magisterial Artificer, to decode them.

Cadi kyl'Ursaal was a Magister, part of a group of magi found in nearly every major city around De Sikkari. These magi specialized in processing the scenes of violent crime and in catching the criminals. Ironically, they bore the name once given to the magi guardians which had themselves been culled from criminals sentenced to death.

That was before Kalla sin'Solidor, Empress Kalla of Dashmar, had set a new standard. The Dashmari had formed their own school to train their magi, the dashhuygin, and revived a lost method of acquiring a protector- that of bonding an elemental in a partnership. Unlike the magisters, who would perish when their magi did, the elementals merely returned to their own plane of existence. Now there were three more Kanlons, in addition to Cryshal and the Dashmari way had become the norm for most magick-users, save Argoth's Technomancers who never used magisters to begin with.

Cadi herself had been trained at Tirithaal Kanlon, located in Ne Ramerides and she was unique in that she had no elemental partner. Though the young Mage had undergone the ritual several times, no guardian had ever presented themselves. Over the years she'd learned to deal with it, but it still hurt. Being a guardianless misfit among the Magi meant being creative. Cadi had taken it upon herself to train with the Harriers of Arkaddia. More than once, those skills had kept her alive in her demanding line of work, where a magick drain could be down-right lethal.

The young, raven-haired Mage finished processing the door and tucked the slides into her pouch. She'd already processed the rest of the outside. With a deft hand she directed her magelight through the wards protecting the scene and into the building. Inside, more magelights bobbed, softly illuminating Cadi's partners patiently working the far end of the room.

"All done. Where do you want me to start in here?" Cadi asked. Rolf's black-furred ears twitched back at her, though the Dashmari Magister didn't look up.

"That end, please, Cadi," Rolf said. "It's too strong for us over there."

Cadi moved the light towards the opposite end of the room. She already knew what awaited her there. She'd been the one to process the body for the Wraiths to take away. The body had lain in a sea of blood, now congealed in a tacky mess upon the floor. Her two Dashmari partners, highly sensitive to scents, could just barely tolerate the thick coppery smell and that only by employing magick to help. Fresh blood brought out the hunting instincts of the wolf-kin.

Starting from where Rolf and Viktor had begun and moving the opposite direction, Cadi began processing the remaining half of the room. Time passed. Rolf and Viktor departed with their own evidence, leaving Cadi in the care of two Crows, as the city guards were called.

Cadi yawned, thankful she was almost done, then paused. Something glittering darkly in the recesses of a corner caught her eye.

"What do we have here?" she mused, holding up an inky black stone. It looked to have been a pendant of some sort, but no chain was in evidence, unless it had been collected by the Dashmari Magisters. Cadi stared at the stone, captivated.

"Lady Cadi?"

The Magister jumped as one of the Crows stuck his head in the door. She absent-absentmindedly tucked the stone in a pocket of her uniform and looked up.

"Yes?"

"Are you almost done, Lady?"

"Almost, Alphonse. I promise."

He nodded and withdrew, leaving Cadi to wrap up her work.

* * *

Cadi stared at the obsidian pendant, wondering again why she hadn't turned it in with the rest of the evidence. She held it up to the light, marveling at the fact that it turned an opaque grey color when held against the backdrop of light. Cadi gasped as the stone grew warm in her hand. Energy boiled within the opaqueness, swirling in a dizzy iridescence that sucked the Mage into its depths.

Let me out! A plaintive, slightly mad voice cried out in her mind.

"Who are you?" Cadi asked.

Come and see. The hypnotic swirl of energy grew stronger and the Mage abruptly found herself in another world, in a dimly lit forest clearing surrounded by dense fog. A small bonfire burned in the center of the clearing and beyond it the shadowed form of someone or some*thing* shuffled forward towards her. Firelight gleamed off glossy black feathers and an ebon beak as the crouched figure moved closer.

Cadi backed away slowly, but the creature didn't seem inclined to chase her. It stopped and cocked its head to the side in a puzzled manner, then straightened to its full height. Cadi's eyes widened as she looked up at the figure that now towered above her own rather diminutive frame. The plumage shifted, revealing a man beneath the glossy coat. He raised an arm overlaid in feathers and Cadi could see paler human fingers below a covering of longer bird talons. He pushed the hood back so that the bird's beak pointed skyward.

At first glance he looked to be Arkaddian. His skin held the same rich coffee tones as the Plains warriors. Though she could see little of his hair beneath the hood, what she *could* see sported more red in it than was typical of the Arkaddians' reddish-brown hair. Scars peppered his face; perfect, purposeful ones near thin lips turned up in a slightly mischievous grin and random ones splashed along his cheeks and forehead, adding to the Arkaddian air. Mismatched eyes of moss-green and mahogany regarded her for a long moment before he tilted his head again in bird-like puzzlement and took another step forward. Cadi took another one back.

"Who are you? Where am I?" she asked, trying hard to keep the fear from her voice.

You still lie on your bed. Your mind is within the stone.

Who am I? Who am I? I am one long lost and forgotten. His voice once again held a slightly plaintive note. *My people are gone. I think… they never were…*

"That is not an answer," Cadi accused. "Why are you trapped here?"

In another world, long ago, I was deemed a threat. I was bound in a volcanic cavern. Bound hand and foot because the Great Ones couldn't face bitter words… Harsh punishment for speaking unpleasant truths… and a propensity for harmless trickery.

4

One day, everything changed. He gave a bitter laugh. *It's ironic actually... they thought* I *would bring about the end of the world. Instead, it was the little ones of Midgard who brought about Ragnarok and the next thing I know, I'm trapped in here. Free of my bonds but still trapped...*

Cadi blinked. "You were trapped in a volcanic cavern? This stone is volcanic glass... obsidian... but who *are* you? And what is Midgard?"

Midgard was the realm of the humans where I came from. There were other realms too. Realms of the giants, realms of the gods, realms of the dead. All connected by the Great Tree. Things are not the same as once they were. I have sensed the presence of some of the Great Ones, but none I knew. And I could not get any of them to hear no matter how loudly I called

As for who I am... I have many names. Sly One, Trickster, Sky Traveler, Wild-fire. A son of giants and blood-brother to the Great Ones. He moved slowly towards Cadi again, his form shrinking so that by the time he stood before her he was no taller than a human male. *My name is Loki and it would be much appreciated if you would release me from this cursed prison.*

"I wouldn't even know where to begin to do such a thing, even if I didn't think it a bad idea," Cadi said.

A bad idea...?

"Who am I to overturn the judgment of the Great Ones?"

Great Ones long since gone. Tell me, Magister, how often in your history's past have people been unjustly imprisoned? Seeing Cadi's indecision, he pressed forward. *I can tell you how to release me. Set me free and I can promise, you will not regret it in the least,* he said, with a look that would melt even an ice mane's heart.

Cadi scowled at him and shook her head. "Why me? Surely others have held the stone before now?"

They couldn't hear me. Some Magi who bore the stone over the years found they could channel their own magick through it and amplify it. They stole my strength, my power…, Loki muttered darkly. *I cannot say why it is that you can hear me where they could not, except that you are the first magickally gifted person to hold the stone who does not have a familiar to call. Perhaps that is what has left your mind and heart open to hear my voice. Please, set me free from this prison.*

Cadi sighed. "I can't believe I'm considering this… Fine, how do I set you free?"

You must shatter the stone.

"That's all? Simply shatter the stone?"

That's all.

"Very well… send me back and I'll set you free."

She twitched a slight grin as his face lit up like a child at Solstice. He snapped his fingers and Cadi found herself back in her own body, gazing at the stone. It was still warm in her hand. The Magister carried it to her worktable and wrapped it in a cloth, then went in search of a hammer from her toolbox.

Tapping the stone lightly with the hammer to mark its place within the cloth, Cadi drew back and swung the hammer against it.

The hammer bounced off, jarring Cadi's arm.

The Magister hit the stone again, this time adding magickal strength to her blow. Again the hammer bounced off.

"Just shatter the stone… easy enough… yeah right…" she muttered, tapping her serryslym ring. The iridescent metal shimmered and flowed out, expanding and covering the hammer. Serryslym was a mage metal that could be willed into different forms. Once the form was taken it became stronger than even diamond. Magisters wore rings and bracers of the material and could form them into myriad weapons, limited only by the Mage's imagination. Cadi swung the serryslym covered hammer again and this time was rewarded by a sharp crack. A final swing fully shattered the stone.

Delighted laughter filled the air and Cadi turned to find Loki standing behind her, still dressed in the raven cloak. She grew alarmed as he swept her up in a hug, twirling her around. His skin was fever-hot against hers, almost too warm to be comfortable.

Thank you!

The demi-deity disappeared, leaving Cadi with the fading sound of laughter. She sighed and shook her head, hoping that she'd made the right choice in freeing him.

* * *

Cadi's eyes flew open and she lashed out instinctively in the dark, willing her serryslym ring into a dagger as she did. Something caught the blade, immobilizing it and a hand grabbed her wrist. Amused laughter filled her mind and the scent of spicy woodsmoke filled her nose. She scowled and conjured a ball of mage-light, illuminating Loki's hooded face.

"*What* are you doing?" Cadi hissed.

"Aww, you're cute when you're irritated," he said, releasing both her blade and her hand. She scowled at him.

"And you're infuriating."

"At times," the raven-man allowed. He settled into a crouch on the floor as Cadi sat up.

"I figured you were gone for good," Cadi said. Loki gave her a wounded look.

"You think too little of me, my dear. I simply wished to stretch my legs so to speak. And go visiting. Alas, I did not manage to find any who knew of me. I seem to be the only one who remembers the old world at all," he said wistfully. "Now I'm back to repay your kindness."

"Go visiting...? You've not been gone that long...," Cadi said sleepily. She checked her chronometer. "I've only been asleep for two hours."

"Time has little meaning for me."

"I see. What will you do from here?"

"Thought I'd stick around a little while. A guardian is what you've wanted is it not?" he asked. Reaching out, he brushed his hand against her cheek. Cadi yelped as pain bit into her ear and her eyes widened as alien chaotic thoughts tumbled into her mind. He withdrew his hand and she reached up to run her fingers over the thin smooth hoop now firmly affixed to her upper ear.

"*I've no people, nor any true home here just yet and certainly I have all the time in the world.*" He gave Cadi a sly grin.

"And how am I supposed to explain how I acquired a guardian overnight?" she asked.

"Tell them you did the ritual yourself. It is possible to carry out alone. You decided to give it another go and were rewarded this time around."

Cadi gave him a skeptical look. "And what kind of elemental are you supposed to be, then?"

His form rippled and shimmered, shrinking down and leaving behind a cinnamon-plumed raven. He fixed a bright eye on her.

"*I think a firecrow works well.*"

"A firecrow. Of course."

"*You don't like this form? What about a fox?*" His form shifted. "*Or a* kitsune?" The fox grew two more tails. "*A sabretooth?*" The *kitsune* became a cinnamon-furred cat. "*Perhaps a falcon?*" The sabretooth became a falcon. Even in these forms the scars on his face were present.

"I'm seeing a pattern here…" Cadi said dryly. "You like the color red. I leave the choice up to you."

The falcon regarded her for a long moment before shifting back to the initial firecrow form.

"*I am a child of fire-giants. The epitaph of 'Wild-fire' is quite accurate. And it is time for you to sleep. We can speak more when you wake,*" he said as Cadi worked to stifle a yawn.

"Is that why you smell like woodsmoke?" she asked as she lay back down. The firecrow cocked its head.

"Do I?" he asked, shifting back to his human form.

Cadi muttered a sleepy affirmative.

"I guess it would be that, then," Loki said. He touched her on the forehead, "Sleep now, my dear. Morning will be here soon enough."

The demi-deity watched the sleeping Mage a long moment, wondering at his choice to be her guardian. Few humans from his previous world had ever woken within him a protective streak. Most had seen him in a darker light. But then, he knew what it was to be a misfit, not quite belonging anywhere. Perhaps this new world would offer him chances the old one hadn't. It was a sobering thought and one he thoroughly enjoyed. They did not know him here. He could reshape himself anew.

The others hadn't understood him at all, nor fully appreciated what he represented. Most only saw that he was *different*, that he was of giant blood, the enemy of the Great Ones. He'd won the friendship and bond-brotherhood of the greatest of the Great Ones and gained access to the realms above, but he'd found no true acceptance there. Those Great Ones had forgotten the truth behind pure chaos, forgotten that it was the only thing that could bring new growth. He'd shaken them from their stupor and they hadn't liked that, not one bit. He'd grown more and more bitter at the stagnation that had overtaken the Great Ones and their refusal to see it and they'd imprisoned him for it.

He shook his melancholy thoughts off and walked to the open window. He shifted form, once more becoming a firecrow and winged his way into the night. Though honestly indifferent to the suffering humans inflicted upon one another, he knew the help Cadi would value the most was in catching her criminals and that was something the demi-deity could certainly do.

He glided on night-dark air, high above the bright lights of Port Jericho, listening. The killer he sought had been the last to hold his prison and he quickly picked up on the man's psychic scent. Marking the hiding place, the firecrow dove towards the ground, shifting in time to lightly touch down. He hadn't shared with Cadi that his prison had been destined for the hands of yet another Mage, likely one who had heard of its amplification properties. The cutthroat he sought, name of Tarlin, had no idea of the stone's true value, but he did know that there would be a harsh penalty if not delivered on time.

The demi-deity ghosted towards the ramshackle hut on silent feet and knocked softly. There was a burst of nervous activity from within. The door creaked open and Loki gave an exasperated sigh as a heavy crossbow quarrel thrummed through it. He caught the quarrel in mid-flight and snapped it with a sharp 'crack'.

"Nice try, but you missed." He shoved through the door before the man could get it closed again and pushed into the filthy room beyond. The man lunged at him, slashing wildly with a knife. Loki caught it as easily as he had Cadi's knife and wrenched it from the man's grip, flinging it out into the night.

"You killed a man last night," he growled. "You left behind a very valuable stone. A stone you were supposed to bring to a certain client. Tomorrow. They will be highly displeased you let it slip through your fingers."

"There's no way I can get it back," Tarlin snarled. "By now it's in the Magisters' Vaults."

"Actually, it's not. Not yet. I can tell you how to get it back. For a price…"

Skycity of Port Jericho, 10000 ft above the Aryth Ocean, Year of the Jade Bull, 2114 CE

Cadi woke to find the firecrow perched in her open window, feathers fluffed against the early morning chill. She shook her head, wondering how he could possibly be cold given the heat he radiated.

"Good morning."

"*Good morning, my dear.*" The crow cocked its head, watching out the window. Cadi could still feel his thoughts, though they were greatly subdued. She reached up and ran her finger over the hoop, marveling yet again at the change in her life.

She stood and yawned, collecting a new uniform for the day. Wandering into the washroom she suddenly became acutely aware of her new guardian's presence and self-consciously locked the door behind her. Dry laughter filled her mind at the sudden anxiety.

"*If I meant you harm, the lock would not stop me.*"

"*You aren't helping,*" Cadi hissed. More laughter in her mind.

"*My dear, I have no intentions whatsoever of bringing any harm to you nor allowing any harm to befall you. Upon that you have my word.*"

He fell silent as Cadi washed and dressed. She paused a moment to regard her reflection in the mirror and her hand went once more to the hoop in her ear. It was, she realized after a moment, crafted of seamless obsidian. When she emerged from the washroom Cadi found the firecrow still watching out the window.

"*What perfect timing. You are about to have company. A quiet thief through the back,*" Loki said. The firecrow fluttered to her shoulder as Cadi turned the serryslym to a long-bladed dagger, shielded herself and crept to the back door. Soft scraping sounds and muffled cursing preceded the thief into the house, no doubt the result of his efforts at breaking her wards. Cadi found the fact that he could breach them surprising in and of itself. The thief in question rounded the corner and pulled up short to see Cadi waiting for him. Snarling in frustration, he raised the heavy crossbow he carried, releasing the quarrel.

It struck Cadi's shield hard enough to stagger her back and giving the man enough time to pull a long dagger from his belt. The Magister hissed out a soft breath and the packed earth floor beneath the man's feet shuddered and shifted, turning to viscous muck. He sank in to his knees and Cadi turned to floor to solid stone, trapping him. She finished the job by binding his upper body in coils of air and liberating the crossbow.

"You were supposed to be asleep!" the thief accused. Cadi gave him a dry look and brushed her fingers over the Magister's pin on her collar, sending a mental call for help. Jupiter answered in the affirmative, assuring her that Crows had been dispatched.

"Obviously I'm not. Why are you here?"

Tarlin bared his teeth at her. "Why should I tell you, Magister? It would make no difference in your treatment of me."

"Suit yourself. We can wait for the Crows to get here."

The firecrow tightened his claws into Cadi's shoulder.

"*I think you'll find this find upstanding gentleman is the killer you and yours seek, my dear. He was the last to hold my prison and that is what he seeks now.*"

"*And how did he know to look* here?" Cadi asked.

"*I told him, of course. I would not have let him harm you.*"

"*Why not just tell me where he was?*"

"*As of the moment you have no real evidence that would have pointed you to him. His 'employer' has charmed him. The finger- prints you found, none of it, would lead you to him, but a mind- read will give you the truth of the matter and now you have the grounds for it. Further investigation will reveal his deceptions.*"

Sounds at the front door took their attention and several Crows flooded into the house, followed by Rolf and Viktor.

"You okay, Cadi?" Viktor asked. The elder Dashmari gave her a critical once over as the Crows secured her prisoner. He frowned at the firecrow perched on her shoulder as Rolf undid the magick holding the man to the floor.

"I'm fine, Viktor, thank you." Cadi smiled at the grizzled wolf. Since they had become partners a few years ago, Viktor had be- come very protective of her. "Rolf, go with them please. Do a mind-read on this gentleman and a scan for illusory magick."

The younger Dashmari gave her a puzzled look but nodded.

"Will do, Cadi." Rolf herded the Crows, together with their prisoner, out the door leaving Viktor alone with Cadi.

"I see you have a familiar now," Viktor said. "I wouldn't have pegged you for a flame elemental. Your temperament leans to- wards earth and water."

Cadi winced. In most cases, a Mage's familiar came from an el- emental realm close to the Mage's natural proclivity. The Dash- mari's own familiar, Luther, an earth elemental in the form of a sleek hunting hound, coalesced beside him and lifted its nose to scent Cadi's new companion. The firecrow made a *reep*ing noise and Luther settled on his haunches, tongue lolling out. The gesture satisfied Viktor and the Magister relaxed.

"Why didn't you ask us for help, Cadi? Rolf and I would have been more than happy to assist you. You took a chance, doing it alone."

Cadi lifted her head and twisted it slightly, baring her throat in the manner of a lesser wolf to the alpha Viktor was. Viktor allowed a small smile to touch his lips as he acknowledged the gesture. Most outsiders still did not know the customs of the Dashmari, despite their greater presence in the world beyond their mountains thanks to Empress Kalla's influence. The one-time Mage and avatar of Amaraaq had forged an alliance with the Argosians and raised the small Dashmari nation into an Empire of its own.

Cadi had taken the time to learn about the wolves when she'd been assigned to the two Dashmari. Rolf, the same age as Cadi, had been trained at Cryshal. Viktor, some six or seven years their senior, was one of the Dashhuygin and had served time with the Donnerkeil as a tracker before coming to Port Jericho. Cadi had no idea what had driven the wolf so far from his homeland. He was silent about it and she didn't pry.

"I apologize, Viktor. It's just… something that was kinda not planned. It is nice though. Nice to not be alone and I can finally carry my full responsibility as a Magister," Cadi said.

"Ah well, what's done, is done. Just remember Rolf and I are always here for you. Come on, let's go see what Rolf's found out."

* * *

A flurry of activity greeted the pair as they arrived at the Magisters' headquarters and two magi healers wearing the colors and crest of House Hilataal pushed past them and hurried down the hall in the direction of the interrogation chambers. Cadi and Viktor exchanged a look and loped down the corridor after the magi. Cadi was fair certain of what they would find and she wasn't to be disappointed.

"What happened?" Viktor barked as Rolf met them. The younger wolf's ears flattened submissively at his sharp tone.

"I saw through the illusions easy enough but when I went to do the mind-read it triggered a hidden spell. Something the likes of which I've never seen before. He started seizing as soon as I began the mind-read. I tried to reverse it and the Crows sent for the healers almost immediately, but it was too late." Rolf paused a moment, letting out a shaky breath.

"I don't know, but it seemed as if the man didn't know this would happen. The look on his face when it started was one of pure shock. Whoever he was someone out there didn't want anyone to share his knowledge. I can... send some samples to Jupiter. If he's in our databases then perhaps we can still learn who he is. Or see if he's connected to any other crimes."

"Well, what's done, is done. You did well, Rolf," Viktor said. "Cadi, do you have any idea why he would have been trying to rob you?"

Cadi shook her head, unwilling to share her own theft of the stone Tarlin had sought with the others. "No, Viktor. No idea at all. It's a fool that tries to rob a mage, though he must have had the backing of a mage himself to have broken into my house. And his manner of death..."

Rolf excused himself as two Crows exited the room.

"The healers must be ready to take the body. I'll go collect the samples now," he said. Viktor gave him a curt nod and shepherded Cadi away to their shared office where new assignments awaited them.

"You'll never guess what Jupiter discovered," Rolf said, as he joined Cadi and Viktor at a small open-air cafe along Jericho's broad central thoroughfare. The two Magisters had spent the morning processing first a suspicious drowning, then the aftermath of a gang eruption.

"What's that?" Cadi asked, far certain of what was coming next.

"The man who broke into your house was our killer from last night," Rolf said. "So that crime's solved at least, though it would have been nice to know the why of both. The body was identified as that of a local merchant. It makes no sense why either of you would have been targeted."

"Guess we'll never know," Cadi said, working hard to keep from laughing as Loki the firecrow edged slowly towards Rolf's plate. His beak darted out, slipping under the inattentive Magister's hand and snatched a biscuit away. Rolf yelped as the firecrow flew off with his prize. Viktor snorted a laugh into his mug of furywine and Cadi lost her own battle at Rolf's bewildered look.

"Bloody crow," he muttered darkly.

"Here, Rolf, have mine. I'm full." Cadi passed him the biscuit from her own plate.

Jerachi Mines, Lower Echelon, East Ward, Port Jericho, Year of the Jade Bull, 2114 CE

"Got somethin' strange 'ere, Cap'n," one of the miners called out. Captain Kellin, Chief of the East Ward mines, stumped over to where three of his miners stood hunched over a 'thumper'. The group had been doing soundings within deepest recesses of the East Ward mines to see if they could be expanded.

Kellin frowned as he looked at the readout. What he saw was impossible. A vast cavern that looked to have been man-made. He touched a button and a three-dimensional image of the sounding resolved itself on the screen. It was a giant maze, replete with numerous dead ends, carved into the rock, its walls rising from floor to ceiling and culminating in a large open area at the center. More puzzling was the fact that the entrance seemed to be blocked by natural stone. The door showed the signature of pyrallym.

East Ward had never shown any signs of man-made ruins. The maze was an anomaly. Even more puzzling was the odd metallic signature that glowed all along the carefully crafted walls. It registered like none of the known metals in the database. No signs of life shone within the sealed chambers.

Kellin looked at the readout again, calculating. Half a day's work and they could be at the entrance. He nodded.

"Call Jackrabbit and Tenger. Have the others ready to place struts behind us. Let's get to work, boys and see what we've got here," the Captain barked as he shouldered his own equipment and slipped the breathing mask over his face. He was joined shortly by Jackrabbit and Tenger, likewise bearing the vaporization equipment and wearing breathing masks. The rest of the miners fell back several feet, slipping masks on as well, ready to shore the tunnel the three diggers would be carving out.

"Halt!" Kellin called out. He shut his equipment off and waited for the dust to settle. There was a soft whine as his companions turned off their equipment as well. Behind him, Kellin could hear the others, busy placing struts along the newly excavated tunnel.

Slowly the thick rock dust cleared enough for the Captain to make out the faint outline of a metal door crafted of dark green pyrallym. Pyrallym chains held the door closed.

"What is this place," Jackrabbit whispered in a low voice. The big miner didn't spook easily, but it was clear from his tone that this place, sealed away far beneath the skycity, made him nervous. Kellin grunted and stepped closer to the door, squinting in the murky half-light. He unclipped his lamp and held it closer to the doors, revealing an inscription etched into the dark green metal. Kellin ran his hands over the writing, his frown deepening. It was Archaic Ekkitaran. Miner the Jerachi Artificer might have been, but archaeology was his first passion and he had a love for ancient Ekkitaros. But there were no known Ekkitaran ruins on any skycity. Kellin peered closer, trying to decipher the inscription.

"Herein… dwells the Bull of Minos… the Great Devourer. Open not the… Labyrinth's Gates…, lest misfortune befall… Jericho's… children once more."

"What does that mean?" Tenger asked.

"I have… no idea," Kellin said, replacing his lamp. "Jerry, bring the sounder. Double-check those readings. Verify there are no life signs."

"Aye, Cap'n." The miner who'd been taking the soundings earlier hurried up with his equipment. After a moment, he nodded.

"All clear, Cap'n. Though what could live sealed away behind there is beyond me. No air flow."

"All right then. Let's open her up."

Jerry gathered his equipment and backed away, leaving Tenger to take his place. The burly miner touched the heavy bracers on his arms and the serryslym flowed and shifted into heavy claws that sheathed his hands. With a grunt of effort, he snapped the chains clean through and they slithered to the ground. He pulled them all the way free and leaned into the door. Kelllin and a reluctant Jackrabbit joined him and finally, with a loud groan and a hiss of escaping air, the door swung inward.

Kellin took the lead, shining his light ahead into the gloom. Only a few steps into the corridor it reflected off a deep blue mage metal the likes of which Kellin had never seen before. Tenger let out a low whistle.

"What *is* this stuff" Tenger asked, tapping it with a claw. He willed the metal back into the bracers and pulled out a serrysllym chisel and hammer. Carefully, and with much difficulty, the miner chiseled off a tiny piece and ran it through his analyzer.

"Unknown composition, closest analog is serrysllym," he said to Kellin. "It looks like we've discovered a brand-new magemetal, Cap'n."

"Sure looks that way," Kellin said.

"Cap'n! I've got life signs. Movement in the central chamber!" Jerry called back. "No… wait… it's gone… Musta been a fluke," he muttered. The group continued their explorations for another half-hour before Kellin called it a day. There were no further instances of life-readings and, in the end, the Captain chalked it up to an honest fluke. It was rare, but it happened. What they did have was a seemingly endless supply of this new metal to begin harvesting the next day.

Within the depths of the Labyrinth's innermost chamber power stirred in the darkness. Dense fog gathered, wafting through the newly liberated tunnels and in the center old bones gathered themselves. Flesh covered bone, fur covered flesh as the wardings of the sealed maze failed and the dweller within resurrected.

A wet nose quivered, drawing in breath for the first time in aeons. A velvet tongue flicked out as the ancient creature yawned, lips pulled back over sharp teeth. The nose trembled again, nostrils flaring as they quested for the scent of prey. The warm, fading scents of humans came to it, carried by the fog and the beast shook its head, snorting in the darkness.

The creature followed the scents through the winding corridors and out into the mine proper, its hunger growing with each step. The fog stayed with it, muffling the sound of heavy hooves and offering a concealment. On through the mine it went, tracking the scents of the miners, til it came to the entrance. Eagerness built, for here the prey smells grew stronger. A lone night guard, tending the East Ward mine entrance. The hunter tensed, shivering with anticipation, watching the oblivious guard with aching hunger.

Closer. Closer. The guard looked up, face furrowing in a frown as the fog curled up the hallway and snaked around him. He lifted a hand to his collar, to a small pin affixed there, but before he could touch it the creature lunged from its obscuring veil, waylaying the hapless human.

Jerachi Mines, Lower Echelon, East Ward, Port Jericho, Year of the Jade Bull, 2114 CE

Cadi frowned as she surveyed the scene before her. Behind her, Rolf lingered further away, a soft chuffing growl issuing from his throat. They ceased after a moment, after the young Dashmari had properly shielded himself, and then Rolf moved up to stand beside Cadi, looking upon the scene in dismay.

The bloody tableau before them was even less pleasant that the one they'd processed just days before. Bits of gore spattered the walls of the mine tunnel in a fine paste, unrecognizable as anything once human or even living save for the rich iron scent that even Cadi could smell.

"Are we even sure this is human…" Cadi muttered.

"Yes…" Rolf croaked, a faintly queasy look upon his face. "Something else there too… Something I can't place…"

The only reason the Magister had walked into the mine without shielding first was to make precisely such a judgment call. Cadi felt sorry for the young wolf, glad that her own sense of smell was not nearly so exquisite.

"Whatever… whomever… it was… it looks like they just… vaporized. It takes strong magick to do such and there is no residue of magick," Rolf said.

"Explosives?" Cadi asked.

"No bitter scent."

"Could you still smell it under all this?" Cadi asked, though she already knew the answer. The wolves' had an exceptional sense of smell, far better than that of most people and Cadi could sense for herself that there was no hint of magick in the area. Rolf nodded.

"The miners use a vaporizer to clear the tunnels."

"Would have been cleaner, had that been the case and again, no magick," Rolf pointed out.

"Well then, let's get to work." Cadi said.

For some time the pair carefully processed the messy scene deep in the Jerachi East Ward mines. Viktor was out, questioning the miners who worked this sector. He joined them after a time, with no encouraging news, but the pair gratefully turned from their work to hear what the Magister had learned. His ears twitched back in an odd flick as he walked up and Cadi frowned, a stray thought wandering through her mind in a detached sort of way before disappearing.

"Night shift guard, Jerrol, came on duty at dusk. He called in no strange activity. The gate guards report no one entering the premises after Jerrol. However, Captain Kellin, the one in charge of the East Ward mines, tells me they opened up a whole new section yesterday. Quite the interesting find. Man-made ruins sealed within solid rock, impossible as that might be. Seems they found a whole lode of an as yet unidentified mage metal in the new section. Kellin's willing to guide us there. The sooner we clear his mines, the sooner the miners can get back to work."

Viktor helped them finish processing the scene, then Viktor had one of the Crows bring Captain Kellin in. The big miner led them through the mines to the Labyrinth entrance. The Magisters pushed the doors shut again, studying them. Viktor frowned as he puzzled out the inscription. He turned back to Kellin.

"Do you know what this says?" he asked.

"Aye, that I do," Kellin replied.

The wolf's frown deepened. "And yet you opened it?"

"No signs of life. We checked. No signs of magick either. I have sent word to Cryshal regarding our find of Ekkitaros ruins and to both Cryshal and Libernaath of our new ore find. I put our economic interests first. This find will be a great windfall for our city. A very great one. A brand-new mage-metal? I don't think I need to remind you, we could use the revenue, Magister."

Cadi sighed. The Captain was right. Such a discovery would be a great asset to the failing skycity. Things were getting worse and each day found new atrocities for the Magisters and the Crows. Cadi's current assignment was a prime example of that. "Will you lead us in, Captain?" she asked. "We should still check things out."

Kellin grunted and motioned for them to follow. Bobbing magelights surrounded the Magisters, though the Captain used only his miner's lamp. True to the mining chief's words, the Labyrinth held nothing except an abundance of the dark blue mage metal. It grew thick in the tunnels. Not too far in, the corridor was almost completely blocked. Even Cadi, the slimmest of the group, couldn't fit through the narrow gap. Surely a killer strong enough to overpower the guard couldn't have fit through either. Cadi whistled softly.

"There's a ton of this stuff here."

"Aye. So there is. Like I said, Magister, it's a windfall. The closest thing to it is serrysllym. For all we know, its properties could be greater than the serrysllym. Tenger and Jerry are processing the samples we took last night," Kellin paused a moment, frowning. "Are we done here, Magisters? My men and I have lost half a day's work."

"We're done, Captain. You're free to resume your operations, if you find anything unusual, anything at all, please let us know." Viktor said. The burly miner nodded to the elder Dashmari.

"Thank you, Magister. We'll be sure to do that," Kellin rumbled.

"What do you think happened back there, Cadi?" Rolf asked. "I've never seen anything like that. The guard, if it was the guard, was completely disintegrated."

"I've never seen anything like it either. I think it'd have to be the guard, with no one else having entered the complex last night. We'll know as soon as the samples have been processed," Cadi replied.

"We know now."

Both Magisters turned to find Viktor entering the office they all shared. The elder Dashmari held a data-pad in his hand. He held it out to them. Cadi took it and scrolled over the information.

"It was the guard. DNA confirms it. No evidence of magick nor traces of the miners' vaporizing equipment found, which Rolf and I already knew. But what's this…," Cadi frowned over the display, puzzling at the readings.

"Some of the trace you collected shows as being similar to bovine, but with significant mutations."

"Cattle?" Rolf asked. "Why would traces of cattle be at our crime scene? There are no cattle on Jericho." Cattle only existed on the far continent of Barsyn, far across the Aryth Ocean and the Shadow Sea.

"Nor many places that use bovine leather, but this was no ordinary cow," Viktor said.

"Wait… what was it the inscription said on the doors in the mine? *Herein dwells the Bull of Minos, the Great Devourer. Open not the Labyrinth's Gates, lest misfortune befall Jericho's children once more.* Bull of Minos… is someone trying to bring the threat to life..?" Cadi's voice trailed off.

"But the only ones who know of the inscription are the miners. We know their equipment wasn't used," Rolf said.

"And they all have verifiable alibis," Viktor said. "They all checked out."

"What if they did let something out?" Cadi asked.

"Perhaps it was unwise to have opened the doors, but Kellin had his team check for magick and check for life. There's no telling how long the maze had been sealed. And it's full of mage-metal. If something had still been alive within, it would have to be smaller than even you, Cadi, to have gotten through," Viktor rumbled. Cadi nodded.

"True. The maze is cluttered with the new mage metal. It just seems an odd coincidence that the inscription should mention a bull and then we find traces of bovine at our crime scene. I've found most 'coincidences' rarely are... and what of the mutations?"

"Well, that is something we can't solve today. It's been a long day. Let's get some rest. I'll be working nights for the next few days. Levett will be working with you two," Viktor said. Cadi and Rolf nodded. It wasn't unusual for the Dashmari to switch his working hours. He did so every few weeks, give or take.

"What do you think of all this? Is it possible that there was something alive down there?" Cadi asked the firecrow perched on her shoulder.

"*I checked, my dear. There was nothing alive down there, but there was a taint to the air. A blood-taint. Sacrificial magick was done there once.*"

"We didn't find any traces of magick," Cadi said.

"*That doesn't surprise me. It was the magick of the world I came from. Something I haven't come across in this realm before, but I remember it. The central chamber of the sealed section reeked of it. It is good you cannot taste the remnants of such magick,*" Loki said.

"But that magick was not in the murder scene?"

"*Not that I could tell. The psychic scent from the inner chamber had filled the mine though. I suppose it is possible that it could have been hiding a newer scent, though your people know nothing of the magick of the world I came from. Many different magick-workers have held my prison-stone and none used the magick of the old world,"* Loki said.

"Tell me about the world you came from?" Cadi asked in a drowsy voice, before taking another sip of her fury wine. She held the glass up so that her companion could dip his beak in. The pair were back at Cadi's home. Dinner was done and they sat snugged before a fire in the hearth-room. Loki *reeped* thoughtfully.

"*Where to begin…*"

"What were the people like?"

"*What were they like… what were they like…? They relied more on technology. Just technology… not the science-magick of the Argosian nation. No… no… They had forgotten the old ways of magick. Scoffed at it, scorned it mostly. There is a balance to this world that is gratifying. You know how to live with the land and the magick, rather than contaminating it.*

"*Most of the humans of the world I came from had all but forgotten the Great Ones, the deities of their ancestors. Oh, there were a few that remembered who we were, who paid a homage to the Great Ones. Some even to me,"* Loki said, a wryness to his voice.

"*But most… they had forgotten. They worshiped one they called God, they elevated one of us above all the rest. There was little room left for contemplation of the rest of us.*"

"But… were the gods not tied to the lands, as they are here? Was there no pride in knowing who you belonged to?" Cadi asked. It was a fascinating concept for her, something completely alien and a little frightening. Here, all lands had their own deities and all of the deities got along, none better than the others. And all things- the land, the people, the deities-, all things were born of the One, which was revered, but not worshiped exclusively.

"Yes… we were tied to the lands, mostly, but we were also tied to the people and travel was so easy by then that people from all lands mingled quite freely. The people had lost their pride though, in belonging to the Allfather, or to Lord Lugh, or to Ares or any of a thousand others. And some… didn't forget, but invaders took their pride from them. They were punished for keeping to their Great Ones. The believers of the one God… well… they couldn't even get along either. There were three major groups. One went out of their way to destroy belief in any deity but their own. Pride in the Great Ones diminished greatly.

"It seems… that is why those humans from the other world lost the love of the land. They lost their way… Then came Ragnarok, the Sundering … Things changed… and that world is no more."

"That seems a rather sad way to live… cut off from the land… with no tolerance and respect for another's customs and beliefs. To be cut off from a close connection with the land's patrons. Not that we have the latter here… not Jericho…" Cadi's voice trailed off and she grew quiet, staring into the flickering fire. Cadi had been born in Kymru and she still retained the ties to the patrons of her homeland, but she'd often felt a measure of sadness for those born Jerachi. Port Jericho had no patron deity, a fact oft said to be the cause of the utter lawlessness surrounding the skycity. It was a transient population of mercenaries, thieves, and grifters mixed with those who ran the gambling dens, the distilleries and the infamous Firefly Alley. This was a place you came to to be forgotten.

Cadi had settled here because she'd wanted to make a difference. It took every ounce of skill that the Magisters could muster to keep things on the skycity stable. They fought an uphill battle every step of the way. Cadi sighed. Jericho was what it was. No use being unhappy over things one could not change. The pair sat quietly for a while longer, before Cadi finally retired to bed. After his charge was safely asleep, Loki disappeared, off to hunt for clues that might help the Magister.

* * *

There was another hunter abroad that night. A pair of emberlight eyes watched from the shadows of a side-street in Firefly Alley. A low snort, unheard over the hustle and bustle of the rowdy crowd. The hunter drank in the energy of the pleasure district like a rich wine. Scents of despair and hopelessness set the wet nose to quivering in anticipation, but activity was still high. The time was not yet right. The hunter watched and waited, full of patience.

Midnight passed to early morning before the pleasure houses began to close for the day. The crowd thinned until there were few people on the streets. Here and there, drunken patrons were passed out on the streets themselves, obviously visitors to the skycity. No sane Jerachi citizen would be caught in such a dangerous position. As the house lights began to wink out, other hunters crept forward, eager to take advantage of the carelessness of the hapless tourists.

A scruffy boy, one of Jericho's many orphans, darted forward to rifle the pockets of one of the bodies littering the streets. Orphans such as this boy were taken in by one of the territorial thief clans or mercenary groups if they were lucky. The more unlucky of them might end up as denizens of Firefly itself. His thieving complete, the scruffy boy moved on to his next victim, bringing him closer to the watcher in the alley. The boy looked fearfully over his shoulder as he moved from incoherent body to incoherent body. He passed before the opening to the opposite alley and yelped as a hand darted out and grabbed his arm.

"Turn it over, rat," a voice growled.

"No, Tomas! I need this! They'll kick me out if I can't earn my keep," the boy protested, struggling weakly. Another boy, stocky and muscular, though only a few years older, slunk from the shadows, twisting the younger boy's arm painfully.

"Not my problem, rat. Turn it over or you won't have to worry about earning your keep."

With another whimper, the boy turned over the spoils of his night's work. Tomas smirked, shoving the boy back down the street the way he'd come. The watcher's eyes remained on the older boy, Tomas, as he swaggered away. Mist gathered, muffling heavy footsteps. Slipping from shadow to shadow, accompanied by the mists' gauzy concealment, the hunter followed the over-confident bully down the street.

Eventually, Tomas turned down another long alley, to the satisfaction of his hungry stalker. The hunter increased its pace, drawing closer. Tomas' movements grew more agitated, his fear building and filling the hunter's nose like a rich bouquet... Tomas glanced back over his shoulder several times, but saw nothing more than the thick, gathering fog common to Jericho's nights and early mornings. Jericho's magnaberms, the lucavite-rich areas responsible for keeping the skycity aloft, kept it above the Aryth Ocean and the vortex-field drew up copious amounts of water vapor.

Heart thudding, Tomas threw caution to the wind and began to run down the dark alleyway. He only managed a few paces. Ravenous, driven to frenzy by the lad's growing fear, the hunter lunged from the mist.

Firefly Alley, South Ward, Port Jericho, Year of the Jade Bull, 2114 CE

"Another one?" Cadi asked with a yawn. It was so early in the morning the sun was only now thinking of rising. She and her partners had been summoned to Firefly Alley, in South Ward where they had been confronted with a scene much akin to the one they had processed yesterday. A fine layer of gore was spattered across a patch of alley, accompanied by a littering of coins, pouches and other trinkets purloined from unlucky tourists. That the stolen items still remained at the scene said a good deal about the superstition with which even the harsh denizens of Jericho held the bizarre crime. Nothing remotely 'human' was left. Cadi wished she had Loki's guidance, but her new guardian had been gone for most of the night. She didn't know where he had gone or when he would be back, but she wished he could tell her if the same residue of old magick was present at this scene as well.

"Well, at least we have one possible witness," Viktor said. "He's with Malitha, the Mistress of Bella Luna. A street waif, scared half out of his mind. It was the Mistress who called the Crows." The Dashmari led the pair back up the alley, now cordoned off by vigilant Crows who were keeping well away from the grisly remains. They walked around the corner and came to the door of Bella Luna, one of the pleasure houses whose walls bordered the alley. A handsome man, who could have been a bodyguard or could have been a firefly himself, greeted the Magisters, escorting them inside with wary watchfulness. He guided them to a back room, where a beautiful raven-haired woman and a scruffy boy wrapped in a blanket waited. The boy looked haunted and ill. He flinched away as Cadi knelt down to his level.

"It's okay, lad," she said soothingly. "It's okay. My name is Cadi. What's your name?"

"Eban, Lady Magister," he said fearfully.

"You have no need to be afraid of me, Eban. We need your help. Can you tell me what you saw?"

Eban shrank back, wrapping the blanket tighter around himself. His voice shook when he spoke again.

"It took Tomas... it came out of the fog and snatched him away."

"Who is Tomas?" Cadi asked.

"I was working... Tomas threatened me... he took my stuff." Eban looked miserable. "If I come back empty-handed, I'll be in trouble..," he whimpered.

"What took Tomas, Eban?" Rolf asked, kneeling down beside Cadi. Eban's eyes flicked nervously to the young Dashmari before returning to Cadi.

"I don't know... it was big, but the fog concealed it. I was following Tomas. I hoped to get my stuff back... but then the creature came from the fog and snatched him away. He didn't even have time to make a noise. It just took him and then... they were both gone...and... and... then there was just blood everywhere, but no Tomas..," Eban lapsed into shuddering sobs and Malitha stepped forward to comfort him.

"Stefan heard the young one screaming in the alley. When he saw the mess, we called the Crows."

"Against my better judgment," the man growled. "We can take care of our own." Stefan lounged in the doorway, still watchful. Cadi regarded him for a long moment. He flashed her a feral smile that promised many things and the Magister realized that he was both a guard and a firefly. Some mercenaries earned income turning tricks in the pleasure quarter when not on a job. Their pay was a place to live and to keep all of the money they made in working for a house. Most of the mercenaries who lived and worked such had grown up within the Alley.

"Why did you call us then?" Cadi asked. Stefan scowled, then shuddered visibly.

"There is a wrongness to this. I went looking. It doesn't do for us to have people murdered here. We get our business attracting people, not scaring them off.

"But… I found nothing. There was no trail. Nothing to follow, either forwards or back. There are no tracks. No evidence of any kind. It takes magick to find a killer who uses magick."

"What makes you think magick was involved?" Rolf asked.

"What else do you call it when a killer pops in, leaves a mess behind, yet no body and no trail to follow, then disappears? That sort of mess? Shoulda been a trail to follow of some sort. I'm a tracker. There was no trail. See for yourself."

"Stefan also has a sensitivity to magick," Malitha said.

"Do you now?" Viktor rumbled. Stefan scowled at the Mistress, but nodded.

"Aye. I do. Father was a Mage. I didn't get the magick, but I have a gift for sniffing it out. Comes in handy for my job."

Cadi had already seen for herself that there was no trail and she had to agree. It seemed more and more likely that some sort of magick had been involved, both here and in the mines, yet the Magisters could detect no evidence of magick. She said as much and earned another scowl from Stefan.

"Not all magick is the same," he said in a flat voice, then smiled sweetly. "Perhaps you aren't looking hard enough. There's magick there. It is unfamiliar to me, but it's there. Dark and heavy it is, but the magick sign is the same. Only there in that one area. There's no trail to follow at all. I can sense different kinds of magick too. The magick used by the Magi of the Kanlon, the Technomancers, the Dragon Priests, the Raven Mages, the Dashuygin, it's all different."

Rolf regarded the firefly for a long moment, his ears twitching.

"You are... half Dunne'kaa. Your father, if I'm not mistaken."

Stefan gave the Magisters another feral grin and this time Cadi could see the points to his teeth, the canines longer than a human's would be. He brushed aside his hair, revealing the fluted ears distinctive to the Dunne'kaa and the Shulonshi of Barsyn. The firefly's hands were gloved, hiding the sharp claws that were another mark of the people of the Dragon and the Raven.

Cadi turned her attention back to Eban, who had calmed somewhat. "Do you remember anything else, Eban?"

"I... it... the creature. It looked big... tall." He pointed to Stefan. "It was... twice tall as him. I... remember seeing horns... a horn... like an aurochi. And it made noises, snuffling noises... like a dog looking for food."

"Horns like an aurochi... Horns like a bull, perhaps?" Cadi mused. She exchanged a brief look with Viktor. The Dashmari had a grim expression.

"What does a bull have to do with anything?" Stefan muttered. "There are no bulls on the skycity."

"Perhaps nothing," Viktor said. "Tell me, Stefan, would you be willing to help us, with pay of course. Your ability to sense the magick would be a big help," the Dashmari asked.

"Of course," the tracker replied, inclining his head in acknowledgment. "For a price. Should you need my help, send a runner for me here."

"That won't be necessary," Viktor said, reaching into his pocket. He pulled out a small pin-comm like the ones the Magisters and Crows wore. With a few soft muttered words, he activated the badge and made to pass it to Stefan, who shook his head, wary and suspicious.

"I don't need the Magisters keeping tabs on me," he said.

"Please, take the comm. It will make things easier. I've tied the badge to only myself and my partners. We'll not interfere with your… extracurricular… activities."

Stefan reached out and took the pin-comm from Viktor. With another scowl, he affixed it to the inside of his shirt collar, then flipped the collar back down, hiding the small badge. He noticed Cadi's puzzled look.

"Don't need those around here to know I'm working with you, now do I? Be bad for business."

Cadi said nothing, but raised her eyebrows in an accepting gesture. Of course the firefly would wish to hide his affiliation with the Magisters. She was surprised that they'd secured his cooperation as easily as they had, but his assistance would make a difference if he could track magick that they could not. Cadi had heard that about the Dunne'kaa and the Shulonshi, that they had a greater sensitivity to different forms of magick than did most Magi, even if they could not use magick themselves.

"*The answer to your question is yes.*"

Cadi flinched slightly as her guardian's voice filled her head.

"*What?*" she asked.

"*There is a faint scent of the sacrificial magick present at this scene as well. Either your killer is saturated in it from the mines, or they are tied to it some other way. I am surprised the tracker can pick up on it. Most impressive.*"

"*Where have you been,*" she hissed. Faint amusement filled her mind through the mental link.

"*Trying to find answers for you, my dear. Something about the maze sealed away in the mine had been tickling the edges of memory.*"

"*And did you find anything?*" Cadi asked.

"*A bit of something, perhaps. A scrap of memory from my own world. Crete, Minos, a legend about a labyrinth and the fearsome creature sealed within. They called it 'minotaur'. Bull of Minos, it means and the legends, if I recall correctly, tell of human sacrifices to this creature. It fits, my dear, though I do not know if this is the same creature. If it is, it's a being from a world long lost, just like me.*"

"*Well, I can't tell my partners that… Beings from a world that we know nothing of. Can you remember anything about this creature that might help us capture it?*" Cadi asked.

"*Not off-hand, but you'll be the first to know, should I remember.*"

Cadi turned her attention back to Viktor, as the wolf was finishing his arrangements with Stefan. The Magisters left Bella Luna, returning to the crime scene in the alley, where they spent the better part of the morning processing.

Shadowylde Lane, Hunters' Quarter, North Ward, Port Jericho, Year of the Jade Bull, 2114 CE

Rain poured down, wet and miserable. Riven glanced over his shoulder for the third time in as many minutes. The grizzled assassin couldn't shake the feeling he was being followed. Years of keeping to the shadows had taught Riven to move easily in them and plenty of attempts by others to kill him had taught the draakeen hunter what it felt like to be the prey. Riven froze, melding into the darkness along Shadowylde Lane. He waited in the rain, watching back the way he'd come, hoping that his stalker would reveal himself. Ten minutes passed, fifteen, twenty. Riven waited thirty minutes in all, but saw hide nor hair of anyone who might have been shadowing him.

Shrugging, the draakeen started moving again, keeping against the walls. He still had the nagging feeling that someone was following him, but it was fainter than before. Still… better safe than sorry. Riven followed a circuitous route as he headed back to Draakengaard. His commander wouldn't thank him for leading someone straight to their base. No one found the draakeen. If they were needed, they found *you*. Riven grew edgy as the feeling of being watched crept over him again. The rain had stopped and fog was filling the night. Riven hoped to find better cover with it. He turned and slipped down a narrow alley off of the Lane. The feeling grew stronger, filling Riven with wariness that was quickly turning to terror. From the fog behind him, a low growly snort came and a snuffling, sending shivers through him. The draakeen, normally quite calm in the face of danger, finally spooked and ran down the alley, going deeper into the growing fog. Heavy, muffled footsteps sounded behind Riven, coming closer. Slipping a pair of daggers from his sleeves, the draakeen backed against a wall and turned to face his assailant. The sound of footsteps ceased and another low growl rolled through the fog.

"Well come on, then. Let's get this over with," Riven snarled. Another growly snort answered him and a shape moved within the fog. A huge shape, far larger than the average human. What looked like horns spiraled out from the sides of its head. Riven didn't have time to make a sound before his stalker lunged, enveloping him in an unearthly inky mist, darker than the fog that now filled the alleyway.

* * *

A week had passed since the as yet unsolved murder in Firefly Alley. Cadi had been hoping that it would be the last, but no such luck. She sighed as she surveyed the scene, just off the main of Shadowylde Lane.

Shadowylde Lane was in the Hunters' Quarter, the area of Port Jericho where the assassins' guilds, and the shops that catered to them, were located. Cadi could almost feel the mistrustful gaze of myriad unseen people, resentful of the Magisters' intrusions. Cadi pulled her jacket tighter, as the strong winds quite common to the skycity, screamed through the narrow alley, kicking up a scattering of debris... including parts of their crime scene.

It was the same as before. The walls and ground were covered in a fine misting of blood and gore, only this time it was partially washed away by early morning rains and scattered by the winds. Two daggers lay abandoned next to the wall. Cadi bent down to inspect the daggers more closely. They were good quality, crafted of narrylym, with a stylized dragon for a hilt. She was surprised they hadn't already been snatched up, but, like the purloined goods at Firefly Alley, the daggers hadn't been touched, no matter how valuable they may have been.

"Viktor, look at this," she called. Cadi had recognized the daggers as having belonged to a member of a specific hunter's guild. The Dashmari walked over, crouching down beside her.

"These daggers… Our victim was a draakeen," Cadi said, pointing to the daggers. Viktor grunted, touching one with a shielded hand.

"The Dragon's assassins don't die easy." Cadi and Viktor both turned as Stefan came up behind them. "And he won't take kindly to this. I'd hate to be the killer, if the Dragon finds him first."

"We'll need to talk to him," Viktor said. "The draakeen's last assignment may give us clues to who killed him. Do you know how to reach this…? Dragon?"

Stefan snorted. "You don't find him. He finds you. You may wish to visit the Wyvern's Roost, here in the Hunters' Quarter. It's one way to get a message to Draakengaard, but I doubt you'll get a response, unless it's the body of your killer delivered to your doorstep."

"I'll take that, at the moment…" Cadi muttered. Stefan smirked at her.

"Magisters happy for a hunter's help? What's the world coming to," he asked. Viktor and Cadi ignored his taunt.

"What about this scene?" Viktor asked. "Do you sense the same magick?" Cadi already knew the answer. Loki had confirmed the same blood magick when they'd first arrived.

The mercenary scowled at them. "This place reeks of it, just as the other one did. Foreign magick, unfamiliar magick, but only in this area. Not leading up to it from the Shadowylde end. I'll check the rest of the alleyway," Stefan said and moved off down the small street.

Cadi and Viktor began to process the site. Rolf joined them, stammering apologies for his tardiness. When they were almost done, Stefan sauntered back up, giving them a smart salute.

"Nothing. Same as before. I even checked the surrounding streets. Can I go now?"

Viktor thanked the mercenary and dismissed him. The Magisters gathered up their gear. Processing the site hadn't taken long. After all… they'd had lots of practice over the past few days and the elements had stolen most of the evidence anyway.

"I'll take what we've got to Jupiter. Perhaps he can tease some more clues from this mess," Rolf offered. Viktor took one of the knives from the younger wolf.

"Come, Cadi. Let's visit the… Wyvern's Roost… and see if we can find this Dragon."

The Wyvern's Roost proved to be a tavern located at the end of Shadowylde Lane, butted up against the Rim Wall itself. The drone of airships was louder here, this close to the Rim Wall. The paddocks were in caverns beneath the city proper.

Cadi followed Viktor through the door. Few people graced the establishment this early in the day. A pair of men sat at a table tucked away in a far corner, their heads close together. They looked up as the Magisters came in. They stood, scowling at Cadi and Viktor, before heading up a flight of stairs.

The only other person in the tavern was the barkeep, a pudgy Argosian who was lazily drying a stack of glasses. Pale brown eyes regarded them with mild disinterest.

"Can I help you?" he asked.

"Do you recognize this?" Viktor asked, sliding the dragon knife across the bar. The Argosian gave him a flat look.

"It's a knife, Magister. Surely you could have figured that out yourself?" he replied. Cadi didn't miss a slight twitch of the barkeep's eye. He recognized the knife, the import of it. She also picked up Viktor's irritation. She placed a hand on the Dashmari's arm and stepped up beside him, giving the barkeep a coy smile. Beside her, Viktor growled softly.

"It was found at the scene of a murder, here in the Hunters' Quarter this morning. It seems likely that it belonged to the victim. We'd like to find who owned it, so we can find who killed him. Your assistance would be appreciated," Cadi said sweetly. Amusement ghosted across the Argosian's face and he reached out to pick up the dagger.

"You found only one?"

Cadi shook her head. "No, there was a second. It's in evidence now."

The barkeep turned the dagger over in his hands for several long moments, before putting it back on the bar with a heavy sense of finality. Cadi was sure he was going to brush them off again. Instead, he let out a series of sharp whistles. Within seconds a slender Arkaddian slipped through the door from the kitchen area.

"Nitka, keep an eye on things," the barkeep said. He walked from behind the bar and gestured for the Magisters.

"Follow me," he said and started walking, leaving them to catch up. They followed him to a storeroom in the back of the tavern, with an oddly placed door in it that would seem to lead to the Rim Wall itself. Etched into the door was the likeness of a stylized dragon wrapped around a spiral. The Argosian went to a comm panel beside the door and punched it. After a lengthy conversation in Argosian, none of which Cadi understood, he turned back to the pair of waiting Magisters.

"I need your weapons and your magickal artifacts," he said. "Nitka and I will keep them safe."

"We're not turning over our weapons," Viktor growled.

"You will if you want to go any further. Makes no nevermind to me whether you do or not," the Argosian replied. "Question is- how badly do you want answers?"

"We will still have our guardians, Viktor, and I doubt these people will offer us harm, unprovoked. Seems bad for business," Cadi said soothingly. She unsheathed her daggers, her service pistol and her serrslym ring and handed them to the Argosian. He took them with a faint smile.

"Wise choice, Magister. And you are correct. If you offer no violence, none will be offered to you."

Grumbling under his breath in Dashmari, Viktor likewise relinquished his weapons. Satisfied, the barkeep punched a code into the door's control panel. It hissed open to reveal a staircase of all things.

"Follow the corridor to its end," the Argosian said. Viktor walked through and, with a last glance at the barkeep who now held their weapons, Cadi followed. The passageway, within the Rim Wall itself, went down several feet before leveling out. They walked several more yards before reaching a recessed door that hissed open as they approached it.

The room they entered was large and simply adorned with a scattering of chairs and tables. It seemed to be a common room of sorts, though there was only one person in it at the moment. A shirtless man stood at a desk, his back to them. An elaborate dragon tattoo graced his back, wings half-furled, fore-paws and head hooked over his shoulder.

"Welcome," the man said. As Cadi watched, the tattooed wings rippled on his back, fully unfurling. He stretched the wings out to their full length as he turned to face them. From the front, the dragon's head took up a good portion of his chest. Cadi did a double-take. The man looked exactly like the barkeep they'd just left upstairs, save that he had golden eyes. And wings... the wings were new too. She only knew of one type of magi who could manipulate mage-metals within their bodies and Cadi guessed that was how the wings had seemed to come to life.

"*You're* the Dragon, aren't you? You… you're a Techno-mancer, a rogue one."

"Very observant, Magister. So I am, on both counts. Give me the dagger, katin." He moved towards them, furling the wings against his back. Viktor growled at the man as he approached, a deep, dangerous sound that Cadi had never heard from him before. His ears flattened in an aggressive manner. The Dragon met and held his gaze, matching the Dashmari's growl with a low one of his own, baring teeth as sharp as the Dashmari's, something no mere Argosian had. Madness glinted in the depths of his golden eyes. He made no other aggressive movements, but after a moment Viktor dropped his gaze and twisted his head slightly, the shadow of a Dashmari's submissive gesture. He held out the dagger. The Dragon inclined his head slightly as he accepted it. Cadi was stunned. She never seen Viktor defer to anyone, Dashmari or not. He was an alpha wolf.

"This belonged to Riven, one of my elite draakeen. Where is his body?" the Dragon asked, turning the dagger over in his hands.

"There was no body," Viktor said.

"Then how do you know he's dead?"

After a moment's hesitation, Viktor explained the scene where the daggers had been found and the two similar scenes.

"We're just waiting to get the results from this scene back," Viktor concluded. "What can you tell us about Riven? About his last mission?"

"Nothing," the Dragon said. "What his mission was isn't important to your investigation. Perhaps, if your other two victims had been targets worthy of a hunter, but they weren't. A street kid and a mine guard? They aren't targets worthy of one of our hunter guilds and any hunter, anywhere, is going to come with a hefty price tag."

"What if they were tests, before the killer went after his real target," Cadi asked.

"Unlikely. We settle our quarrels without killing one another and between us, the Hunter Guilds are aware of any new or potential hunters that come to Port Jericho. We have our differences and disagreements, but we share that sort of information. We need no outside competition and we don't take kindly to interlopers. Our watchers at the paddocks have reported no new arrivals in weeks."

"Aren't assassins trained to blend in, to be unnoticed? Wouldn't they be poor hunters if you could spot them?" Cadi asked dubiously. "What if this were a hunter who was... being trained?"

The Dragon grinned, a feral looked that bared sharp teeth. "We *are* trained to blend in, and do so quite well, no matter what flavor of hunter we happen to be. The Guilds' watchers are veterans, well-trained to know how to spot others like themselves. It takes a certain measure of talent.

"As for the training idea... trust me, Magister, if we trained our fledglings with Jericho's citizens you'd have a great deal more unsolved murders on your hands. It's a poor hunter who draws such attention to his killings by vaporizing them. That hardly helps us to blend in. Besides, you mentioned that all of the scenes contained traces of magick. You're looking at the only Jerachi hunter currently capable of using magick." the Dragon said. "Now, if you'll excuse me, I have work to attend to. I'll send Dracos to collect Riven's other dagger. Synmerra, Magisters." He turned, wings flaring out briefly, before rippling back into his flesh.

"Wait," Cadi said. "Why did you meet with us? Reveal yourself to us? What's to keep us from turning you in?"

The Dragon turned, meeting Cadi's gaze, golden eyes boring into hers.

"You intrigued me and you came bearing one of my draa-keen's daggers and news of his death." The Dragon paused, face troubled and when he spoke again, it was in a much softer voice.

"….Each of my draakeen… they are my children. I raised them all, took them in off the streets and trained them. My son is dead. That's a matter for me to attend to. As for why I revealed myself… you would be foolish to turn me in. I sus-pect your companion knows that. I am more than just a Tech-nomancer, Magister. Jericho has been my home before your mother's mother was just a thought to *her* mother. To subdue me, it would take the efforts of those like me and it would tear your city apart. If I survived and you survived, I would come hunting *you*. Now, tell me, is that something you really want?

"I will tell you this, also. By bringing me this dagger, you have made this killer my problem. I don't take kindly to people killing my draakeen. Expect to have your killer delivered to you soon enough. Deceased, of course."

"You're an Old One?" Viktor asked. "A rogue Old One…" He glanced to Cadi.

"No, we'll not turn you in. But perhaps… you would be will-ing to work with us? You may be a hunter," Viktor growled, "but you are a mage with experience… and senses that none of us can match. It may be that you can see something we cannot. I'm willing to give you access to the sites, access to our information."

The Dragon narrowed his golden eyes, considering. "Access I could get, should I desire to. I do not need your… permission… for that."

Viktor growled again, but didn't challenge the Argosian hunter's claim. After a moment, the Dragon chuckled, clearly amused.

"Smart. Well, that's good. I'll help you, kas… but on my own terms and by my own rules," he said, turning to walk to a nearby cabinet. He opened it and pulled out what looked like a pair of pins to Cadi. The Dragon whispered something in Argosian, holding the objects in his fist. Liquid metal welled up from his hand, pooling in his palm as he opened his fist, and covering the pins. There was a muted silvery flash and the Dragon grunted in apparent satisfaction. He held out the pins, in the shape of the dragon and spiral that had graced the doors, to the Magisters. Viktor took one, looking it over. Cadi gave the Dragon a distrustful look, reluctant to take the pin. He chuckled again.

"To contact me," he said. Cadi scowled as she took the proffered pin.

"Why not use one of ours?"

"Do you really think I want you to be able to track my every move? Oh no. Bad for business. These pins will allow me to reach you much faster, should it be necessary."

"How?" Cadi asked, curious.

"He's a jumper," Viktor guessed. He looked to the Dragon. "You've tied these to your own essence."

The Dragon inclined his head, still looking amused.

"But jumping takes a good deal of energy. It's a rare skill for a Mage."

"Aaah, but I'm *not* a Mage, am I? Jumping is still rare among Technomancers, but among the Old Ones it's quite common. Even if the Technomancer couldn't before the Conversion, we usually can after and quite effortlessly. A gift of Master Mercurius and the new body we're given," the Dragon said. "Name's Draccus, by the way."

"You're awfully talkative," Cadi said.

"Perhaps. I've shared nothing you can harm me with. We've already established that your alerting the Empire would be a *very* bad idea. I trust the consequences will keep you from betraying me." He gestured to the doorway. "Synmerra, Magisters. This time for truth. I pray we need not see one another again."

"Likewise," Viktor growled, "Though I doubt that prayer will go answered."

Viktor's words proved true. Over the next month, there were seven more similar killings, most with no witnesses. Those that did have witnesses reported stories much like Eban's, of a large figure hidden in the mist and the hint of horns. Despite the assistance of both Stefan and Draccus, each case was a dead-end. The victims and locations appeared completely random. A guard, a street kid, a hunter, two mercenaries, a firefly, a miner, a distillery work and a pair of Crows. They had nothing in common, nothing to link them together. There was no rhyme or reason to the victims. The only consistency was the vaporized remnants of a body. It was only by the artifacts left behind that they were able to get clues to the victims' identity.

At each scene, Stefan confirmed traces of the same dark magick and each time, the tracker was unable to find any sort of trail. The Argosian hunter had little better luck. His unique body and its particular talents allowed him to find a trail where the tracker had been unable and yet… they still had no leads. The trails Draccus found only led a few yards away the scene before they vanished for him as well. Despite all of the *other* efforts the Dragon had put forth, he'd had no better luck than the Magisters themselves at finding the killer and the longer the killer remained at large, the more surly the Dragon became.

"What are we going to do, Viktor," Cadi asked. "The people are growing paranoid. They're afraid to leave their homes at night. Gods help us if this killer ever strikes during the day."

"Cadi's right. Things are growing more unstable by the day," Rolf added. "The Crows have had to double their patrols… and our own work has increased triple-fold. Too many taking advantage of the unrest…"

"It *is* a city of thieves and mercenaries," Viktor growled. "To make matters worse, the Argosians have responded to the discovery of the new metal in our mines. The presence of the ships and the imperial soldiers isn't helping matters. The Governor hasn't let them into the mines yet and they're getting a little impatient as well."

"Took them longer to come snooping around than I would have guessed," Rolf said.

The three Magisters were in their office at the Magisterial Headquarters. Beyond their cubby, other Magisters went about their business. A panel on Viktor's desk chimed and Jupiter's voice came through.

"Captain Kellin's calling for you. Says he's found something in the mine he says you might want to take a look at. What should I tell him?"

"Tell him we're on our way," Viktor replied. He looked to his partners. "Perhaps he's found something useful."

Kellin met them at the mine entrance, looking haunted.

"We reached the center of the Labyrinth," Kellin said. "Perhaps… perhaps I should just show you what we found."

Viktor nodded an assent and the Magisters followed Captain Kellin through the mines to the great pyrallym doors, whose chains still hung loose. The miners had been busy over the past month and though many side passages were still stuffed with the dark blue mage metal, the main throughways were free. They followed Kellin as the miner navigated the winding passageways with practiced ease, leading them to the Labyrinth's center.

"We reached the center chamber yesterday. Today… we uncovered this," Kellin said, as he led them to a low table in the very middle of the chamber, still partially encased in the blue metal that Kellin was calling 'tryllym'. Strange glyphs and delicate Ekkitaran script decorated the visible parts of the table, along the top and the edges, spilling down the broad supporting base. Closer inspection revealed a deep depression, still mostly hidden. Dark splotches stained the rim, dipping down into the basin. Recalling Loki's story of the 'minotaur', Cadi had the unpleasant feeling that she knew what it was.

"What I can read of it, part seems to be an incantation to summon or recall the 'Bull of Minos' mentioned on the doors, though who or what that would be, I've no idea." Kellin frowned, tracing over parts of the fine script. "And this part… this part tells of sacrifices made to this being, to placate it. This was its home. It roamed these corridors in a wraith-like form, taking a solid shape only to feed. Offerings were sent to wander the Labyrinth." The mining captain walked around the plinth to another cleared patch. "And this… this here describes instances in which this creature was sent out after others… times of war… assassinations… The only time it could leave the Labyrinth."

"A wraith-like creature… that certainly *sounds* like our mystery killer," Rolf said.

"A creature whose magick we can't sense. Captain, can you finish uncovering the incantation please? Perhaps then we can recall that which was unleashed," Viktor asked.

"I sent the others home, once we uncovered the table. I knew you would wish to see it, " Kellin said. He removed his helmet and ran a hand through his short hair, unhappiness lining his already craggy face. "We did this… we let this thing loose… but, there was no trace of magick we could recognize… how could we have known the full truth…"

Cadi felt sorry for the man. The miners had scanned for magick and the room had been sealed and stuffed full of the blue metal. It seemed a reasonable assumption that nothing could be alive in the Labyrinth.

"Call some- " Viktor stopped, ears flicking forward as he caught a sound. He cursed softly. Rolf's ears flicked forward too and his shoulders slumped slightly. Moments later, Cadi and Kellin picked up the noise that had distracted the Dashmari. It was the sound of the city's disaster sirens wailing out a funeral dirge. The Magisters' pins chirped and Jupiter's voice came through.

"*Riots in progress. All Magisters respond. Repeat, riots in progress. Locations- Firefly Alley, Shadowylde Lane, East Ward airship paddocks and North Ward distillery district.*"

"Gods help… that covers the entire city," Cadi breathed, as Loki the firecrow materialized on her shoulder. "When things go wrong, they go *wrong*."

You have no idea, my dear. No idea at all… Things are bad, Loki said. *There was an attack, this time in view of quite the crowd in Firefly. Then another, at Shadowylde. I have no idea how the killer could have gotten from one side of the city to the other so quickly, but both fit the pattern of your killer who vaporizes their victims. This city being what it is… the panic spread like… well… like wildfire.*

Luther materialized beside Viktor as he responded to Jupiter's message. They were to report to Shadowylde. Viktor instructed Kellin to recall his miners and get the table uncovered as soon as possible. As the three sprinted their way out of the mines and headed for Shadowylde, Cadi quizzed Loki about the nature of the 'minotaur' from his world.

"*No… I can't say I recall it every being allowed out of its Labyrinth home, nor any stories that give it as anything other than a being of flesh and blood. A mortal being with a mortal lifespan.*"

"*Then it seems unlikely to be the same creature from your world.*" Cadi sighed, frustrated. So much about this case didn't make sense… but that wasn't for here and now, not with riots to get under control.

Compared to the rest of Jericho, Shadowylde was a walk in the park. The hunters who ruled this part of the city had taken things in hand, calming and dispersing the crowds, cloistering off the scene of the killer's attack. There were already a handful of Crows and Magisters, processing the scene. Draccus met the Magisters when they arrived.

"Figures it'd be the three of you," he muttered. He fixed them with a grim look, golden eyes cold and unforgiving. "I saw it."

"You what?" Cadi asked.

"I saw it, the killer. I was there at the attack. It *is* the mist. That's how it kills. The dark mist gathered, out of nowhere. We had no fog here in Shadowylde tonight. There was a snuffling sound, a glimmering of horns and then the mist enveloped the victim. He didn't have a chance to scream. He was there and then… he wasn't. That's why there's no trace of it. Whatever this creature is, it doesn't maintain a corporeal form."

"That makes sense," Viktor said.

"Basa seite…" Draccus muttered. "*How* does that make sense?"

The Magisters shared with him what they had learned from the mines earlier.

"As soon as Kellin uncovers the inscription, we can attempt to recall this creature. However… there's little guarantee that we could control or contain it."

"Time enough to worry about that when the miners are done, though that certainly makes things much easier." Draccus shifted a bag he carried slung over his shoulder. Settling it on the ground, he pulled out several pieces of equipment.

"After I realized how this creature was attacking, I had an idea. This is a stasis field modulator. I've been collecting them from the various Hunter's Guilds. Most Guilds have only one as they are rather expensive. If we set several of them up we can form a large containment field. Perhaps it would be enough to keep the creature at bay, if it were summoned into the field."

Cadi and her companions took over for those working the scene, freeing them to assist in other parts of the city where riots still raged. The other three wards had been far less lucky than had North Ward, with its Hunter guardians, and Cadi suspected it would be hours before things were effectively calmed throughout the whole of Jericho. They were just finishing their work when Jupiter patched Kellin through to Viktor again. The Captain had called his men back in and they had since managed to uncover the rest of the stone table.

"*Aye, we've uncovered it. You're not going to like what we've found though.*" Kellin answered Viktor's questions. The Captain's voice grew softer. "*To summon the creature, to recall it to the Labyrinth's center, requires a sacrifice, not just blood, but life itself.*"

"Is anything else necessary?" Viktor asked.

"*No. It just requires the offering and someone to speak the words. I... can do that for you. I speak Ekkitaran fluently. There's still the sacrifice to consider... It must be a human life. The wording is very specific.*"

"We'll figure something out. We'll be there soon." Viktor broke the connection with Kellin and contacted Draccus. The Argosian hunter listened while Viktor explained what the mining captain had uncovered. There was a long pause and Cadi thought perhaps Draccus had broken the connection.

"Give me an hour," he said. "I've an idea for the sacrifice. I'll meet you at the mine with the stasis field modulators. We can set the field and summon the creature into it, perhaps find a way to destroy it for good."

Draccus arrived at the East Ward mines just shy of his promised hour. With him came the bartender guard he'd called Dracos. Both Argosians carried satchels. They greeted the Magisters with curt nods.

"Let's get this done," Draccus said. "Lead on."

"You had an idea for the... necessary requirement?" Viktor asked. The Dragon gave him a grim smile, baring his sharp teeth.

"You're looking at 'em," he said.

"But..." Cadi's voice trailed off in a hoarse whisper.

"Look, it needs doing. Are you going to volunteer? Will you drag one of your incarcerated criminals down here and sacrifice them?"

Cadi and Rolf shared a horrified look. Viktor gave Draccus one of deepening respect. He twisted his head slightly, once more acknowledging the Dragon as alpha to him. They followed the corridors through the mine. Draccus let out a low whistle at the great pyrallym doors, with the chains coiled to the side. They entered the Labyrinth, following its winding path to the center. The Dragon chuckled softly as he surveyed the chamber, still partially full of tryllym. He knelt to inspect some.

"My brethren would be frothing to get at this," he said, with a wry grin. "You should turn quite the tidy profit from it." Draccus stood and walked to the center plinth, where Kellin stood. By this point the Captain had sent his men away… away from one danger, but likely into another, since riots still swept the city.

"And you must be the one who set this creature free. It's you I get to thank, that I go to Shae N'Sala this day." Draccus' golden eyes narrowed. Kellin's jaw tightened, but he met the Dragon's fierce gaze.

"We didn't understand. I would offer myself, to end this madness, but I don't know any others within the city who can pronounce Archaic Ekkitaran fluently. Do you?"

Cadi saw the hint of madness in Draccus' eyes again as he laughed. "Indeed I don't. Today is a good day to die!" He clapped his hands together, then shrugged his pack to the floor. "Let's get these set up, shall we?"

They spent the next several moments setting up the stasis field modulators, linking the fields so that they overlapped. Stasis field modulators were Artificer-crafted, designed to set up wards similar to the ones a War Mage might set. They could be adjusted to erect a variety of shields. Cadi had never seen one up close. Draccus was correct. They were expensive pieces of equipment and she was impressed that the Guilds had so many between them. They'd arranged the modulators along the perimeter of the room so that once activated, the linked fields would encompass the entire room. They set each modulator to its maximum capacity and in doing so, enabled several types of shields, each overlaying the other- shields against magick, shields to prevent solid objects from passing through, shields to stop things less than solid. Cadi was hoping they would be enough to hold the creature in, once summoned... that its unique magick wouldn't be able to slip through.

"Well, I think that just about does it," Draccus said.

"How do we keep it contained once we summon it?" Cadi asked. "Or better yet, destroy it?"

"I intend to try mage-fire against it. I know little that mage-fire cannot kill, magickal beastie or otherwise. There are also instructions for a binding on the plinth. I will incorporate that into the summoning. Even if the mage-fire doesn't work, the creature should still be bound within the Labyrinth once more and we can take time to figure out how to destroy it," Kellin said. "It would be best if the three of you went beyond the bounds of the modulators."

Draccus walked to the modulator nearest the entrance and lowered the section of shielding blocking them in. "Out you go, then." One by one, the Magisters filed past him.

"This won't be forgotten," Viktor said. Draccus gave him another slightly mad grin.

"Nope, I 'spect not. I certainly won't forget it."

Cadi frowned at the odd statement as she and Rolf passed through the gap in the shields. She turned to face the Dragon.

"You're brave. I'll give you that," she said and then, more softly, "Thank you." Cadi paused a moment before continuing. "Do you... do you have any last requests?"

"Dos mere, but Dracos here already knows my final wishes. He will see to things." Draccus replied. His look turned sly.

"However… if you're offering… how about a kiss for good luck?"

Cadi rolled her eyes, trying to keep the tears from coming. She'd misjudged this man, this hunter who should have been her enemy. He had honor. She nodded, stepping towards him. "I think I can manage that."

He bent towards her. Up close, Cadi could see the deeper gold flecks in the Dragon's golden eyes. His kiss was gentle but confident. He kissed her a second time, more deeply and Cadi's hand involuntarily tangled in his curly hair. Draccus gave a throaty, pleased growl. Behind her, Viktor gave an impatient one. Draccus chuckled, leaning into Cadi.

"Dos mere," he whispered before stepping back into the chamber and activating the final modulator, sealing Kellin and himself inside and leaving them to watch from the outside. The Dragon carried on a muted conversation with Kellin, then knelt before the Captain, wings unfurling as he did so. Draccus bowed his head and Cadi saw his skin ripple. A gap opened in his back, between the wings.

Cadi could hear Kellin speaking, his words unintelligible. The Captain reached down, thrusting his hand into the bloodless wound in the Dragon's back. Cadi whimpered, though Draccus didn't seem bothered by the intrusion. Beside her, Dracos was murmuring in soft Argosian. Kellin pulled his hand out, clutched in a fist. As he did so, the Dragon's body tumbled forward bonelessly, wings splayed out to the side.

Still speaking, Kellin laid an object on the low table and when he drew away, Cadi could see it was a small square- the chip that contained the Old One's essence, his soul. Kellin willed one of his bracers into a stout mallet and brought it crashing down on the chip, smashing it to pieces.

"Synmerra, friend," Dracos said beside her, slipping back into Common.

Within the chamber, inky fog was gathering. It grew thicker and coalesced into a towering form. The beast walked upright, like a human. It had a massive head, like an aurochi, with long grey horns shading to black at their sharp tips. Shaggy black fur covered its chest. It had human hands, but they were tipped with long claws in place of blunt fingernails and its feet were the heavy broad hooves of an aurochi. Red malevolence burned in its eyes. The minotaur bellowed and Cadi could see that the bovine muzzle was filled with sharp teeth, reminding her of the *ghilan* of Xibalba, whose equine muzzles housed equally sharp teeth. It focused on Kellin and bellowed again.

Kellin collapsed the mallet and raised his hands and in the next instant, the minotaur was encased in purple mage-fire. Mage-fire burned faster and hotter than regular flames. Normally it was a greedy thing, eagerly consuming all it was offered. The beast bellowed again, reverting to fog and extinguishing the flames. The fog roiled against the stasis field, but couldn't go further, stopped by the binding Kellin had created or by the overlapped shields created by the modulators. The fog grew darker. Hidden from sight, Cadi heard Kellin's voice calling out. The fog drew together again, as the minotaur regained its corporeal form. It bellowed at the Captain, even as he engulfed it in mage-fire again. The creature dissolved and this time the fog descended upon the miner. There was a sharp cry and when the beast reappeared, there was nothing left of Kellin but a fine mist and the bracers he'd once worn.

Seeing the Magisters for the first time, the minotaur bellowed and charged them. The field flared bright blue when it hit, but held firm. Rolf yelped as all four scrambled back from the field. The minotaur backed off and charged the field again. The shields held firm once more, but this time a great deal of sizzling and sparks accompanied the bright flash of blue.

"I don't think the field is going to hold much longer," Rolf said, voice shaky with fear. Cadi agreed.

"*Loki! Help us!*" she cried out. In response, a desert hot wind whipped down the corridor, past the Magisters and the hunter. It passed through the stasis shields as if they were nothing and the chamber beyond erupted into an inferno that burned so hot they could feel the heat even through the protective shields. The minotaur's enraged bellow turned into a sharp wail of agony. Clearly, Loki's fire could hurt the beast where mage-fire couldn't. The wildfire burned brighter and hotter, driving the group further away. After several long minutes it winked out. Beyond the stasis field, Draccus' body and Kellin's bracers were gone. There were only dark scorched marks on the floor to suggest where they might have once lain. Of the minotaur there was no trace. The modulators remained unscathed, but Cadi suspected it was more by Loki's choice than their ability to withstand the deity's fires. Something was still moving in the chamber, however. Loki, in his human form, strode from the smoky haze, passing through the shield as if it weren't even there, feathered cape fluttering around him. Viktor growled at his approach. Cadi put a calming hand on his arm.

"Viktor, meet Loki. He's my guardian." Turning to Loki, she said, "Thank you for helping. Is it… gone for good?"

The raven-man nodded. "*It is. There's no more taint of sacrificial magick here. I burned it away, along with the anchors that chained it here. It's gone and won't be coming back, but that might not make no nevermind now. This city is falling apart. The riots are much worse now.*"

The Magisters took off running back to the front. They spilled out of the mine entrance to the sound of the disaster sirens. Throughout East Ward, fires raged and they could see smoke rising from dozens more in the other Wards. A series of explosions knocked Cadi off her feet.

Cadi flinched as more explosions rocked the city. Dracos had vanished in the confusion, once they were free of the mines.

Viktor had checked in, to see where they should head next and the report from Jupiter was grim. The Crows, and the Magisters themselves, had been overwhelmed by the sheer fury of the riots. Beyond the Rim Wall, she could see the looming Argosian flagships. She watched in a growing horror as the lead flagship locked its main ion cannon into firing position. Cadi knew that the Argosian Empire had little use for the tiny skycity with its excessive criminal element, but she couldn't believe they were willing to simply destroy the population.

Come. I can take you away from here. Loki's voice sounded in the Magister's mind and the firecrow winked into existence, shifting to his human form. Cadi shook her head.

"No... no. This is my city, this is my home. I'm not going to abandon it, even if no one else will care that we are all gone. I'm not leaving." She gave a soft, shuddering sigh, thinking of all they had just gone through, in an attempt to protect the city. It all seemed so pointless now.

Loki cocked his head to the side, regarding her for a long moment. He turned abruptly and walked off, disappearing as he did so. Cadi sighed, struggling to keep the tears she wished she could shed from falling. She turned to look at Viktor and Rolf. At least the three would be together at the end. It was a small comfort.

"What... is... that..?" Rolf asked, alarm filling the young wolf's voice. Cadi and Viktor looked to what held Rolf's terrified gaze. Fire spread along the top of the great Rim Wall, a massive curtain streaking to circle the entire city. The flames undulated like a living thing and, as the circle came close to completing, a huge serpentine head lifted up, roaring a challenge to the great flagships. The fire-serpent roared again, spitting laval rain at the lead ship.

* * *

"What in the name of Holly is that?" Commander Barnardsson whispered.

"I don't know and I don't care!" Admiral Salisson barked. "Raze this godforsaken city to the ground!"

"Aye, Admiral. Cannon ready. Commence firing." Barnardsson's voice had regained its professionalism. The gunnery officer snapped out a 'Yes, sir', but before he could activate the ion cannon, the doors to the flagship's bridge hissed open and a man wearing a silvery-grey uniform emblazoned with the Technomancers sigil walked in, accompanied by the *Kraken*'s Chief Technomancer, Alarius.

"I wouldn't do that if I were you," the stranger said. "Stand down or I will *make* this ship stand down. I assure you, you do not want that, Admiral."

Behind him, Alarius shook his head and mouthed the word *'listen'*. Salisson grimaced, but nodded to the gunnery officer who took his hands away from the console.

"What is the meaning of this?" he growled.

"All in good time, Admiral. All in good time. At the moment, you have a more pressing problem." The man walked down into the bridge, past the Admiral and stood facing the windows. He barely acknowledged the liquid fire that pattered off the flagship's shields, his attention fully focused on the serpent filling the view.

Greetings, strange one. I have no quarrel with you. My name is Mercurius, Patron to the Technomancers of Argoth.

The serpent's jaws closed with a sharp snap, the head swaying slightly side-to-side as it contemplated the ship.

I am called Wildfire. I claim this city. It is mine. I will defend it.

I do not know you, Wildfire, nor do I think that truly your name. It fits you well though. A slight grin played across the Great One's face as he regarded the fire-serpent. *Jericho has never had a Patron before. Why do you now claim this city of criminals?*

It can be more than it is. It has been a haven for the outcasts and the misfits. That is all I am now, all I was before as well. I have a chance to be something other than I was. I have no place here, so I will make my own. And I will protect it! At this, the snake reared up, roaring another challenge to the ships.

Peace, brother. I have no quarrel with you. Mercurius turned back to the Admiral, the slight grin still upon his lips. Oh, he liked this one, he did. They could be friends. "Power down the cannon. Back the ships off to twice the distance they are now. Prepare to aid and assist the city. You'll know when it's advisable to send the strike-fighters in."

By this time, Alarius had filled the Admiral in as to who the mysterious man was. Silasson nodded, jaws clenched. The Admiral didn't want to aid the city, lawless abyss that it was, but he wasn't going to defy the orders of the Great One who protected the Argosian fleet. He began barking out his own orders as the man disappeared.

Mercurius reappeared hovering in the air before the fiery drake. The serpent's eyes narrowed and it snorted, smoky tendrils issuing from flared nostrils. A warning rumble built, shivering the Rim Wall with its force. Chunks of rubble and rock, loosened by the serpent's challenges, rained down into the city and the ocean far below.

If you keep that up, you will do Silasson's job for him. The ships are no longer a threat to the city. Please, forgive us. It is not in our nature to use force when peace will work just as well. The Kraken's *admiral was perhaps not the wisest choice to send to this city. His hatred of Jericho is well-hidden, but runs deep. I will negotiate with you on the behalf of my children.*

What I broker, not even the Emperor will negate. You have something infinitely valuable to my Technomancers. What we offer is assistance now and assistance for the future. With the proper guid-

ance of a Patron who cares, I have no doubt at all that Jericho can become a great deal more than it is now.

Will you speak with me and let the ships assist? No strings attached. I promise. Mercurius said.

Very well. We will speak. The firedrake lowered its head to just above the tail, which had started to solidify into darkness. Meter by meter the serpentine body cooled, glowing at points like dying magmal embers. When the transformation finally reached the weredrake's head, what remained was a massive obsidian statue ringing the city entire, the head raised watchfully above the tail, mouth gaped open slightly in a silent challenge.

With a flash and a rumbling crack, the light left the statue's eyes and a feather-clad figure stood perched atop its head. Mercurius drifted down to alight next to the one who called himself 'Wildfire'.

Once his newly-claimed city was safe from the approaching airships, Loki turned his attention back to Cadi and grew alarmed by what he found. His charge was hurt, her pain dulling the link between them.

That speaking will have to wait. Loki said. *My companion is injured.*

Loki disappeared, reappearing where he had left Cadi. He found the mine area in shambles, large chunks of debris littering the area. It was pinned under two of these that he found Cadi, her left arm and right leg fair crushed. Viktor and Rolf were trying to free her, but they were having little luck in lifting the rubble. Cadi herself was unconscious. The Dashmari backed off as Loki approached. The raven-man lifted the boulders that had given the wolves such trouble, carefully setting them aside. He frowned down at his charge. Her life-force was weak, fading quickly.

Loki gathered Cadi's broken body in his arms, the feathered cloak falling around her. Healing wasn't a gift of his. He couldn't save her. He'd saved her city at least, the city she'd refused to leave. He wasn't completely sure it was worth it. Cadi had freed him from eons of confinement and this was his repayment? He was pretty sure that he was the cause of the rubble that had crushed the Magister. Loki was surprised to find tears stinging his mismatched eyes. They disappeared before they could slip too far down his cheeks, burned away by the growing heat of the demi-deity's skin.

Movement from the wolves brought Loki's attention back to the here and now. He looked up to find the one called Mercurius approaching.

Here you are. Mercurius stopped before Loki and knelt down beside him. *She means something to you, yes?*

She does. Loki said. *She didn't want to leave the city. That's what prompted me to claim it. She helped me and I have no way to repay that.*

Perhaps I can help with that. Mercurius took Cadi's limp form from Loki. *You can follow her, yes?* Loki nodded. The link he'd formed with her would let him find her no matter where she went.

Good. We'll see you later then.

"Wait! Where are you going to take her?" Viktor interrupted, protectiveness etched into his aggressive stance. "And who are you? *What* are you?" he asked, turning to face Loki. "You're not a guardian." The Argosian Patron gave the wolf a placating look.

I am going to take her to be healed. My children are good at that. She'll be fine, don't worry. When she is better, you can come and see her. With that, Mercurius disappeared, bearing Cadi's body away with him and leaving Loki to deal with the unhappy Magisters.

You're correct. I'm not a guardian. Well, not the kind you're thinking of. I am the one who just stopped those flagships from destroying this city though.

I am called Loki. I am from a place that no longer exists and I have no home here, so… I decided to claim this city as my home to protect. I regret the destruction I caused, but… Cadi's injuries aside… it seems better than letting the whole city be dropped into the ocean, yes?

"Wait…," Rolf said. The young wolf looked confused. "You mean… we have a Patron now? The Jerachi?"

I mean exactly that. And now we have a city to stabilize. The Argosians will be sending help now. We need to make sure they can land safely, so… let's get to work. As soon as I know Cadi is well, I will let you know.

The Dashmari exchanged a look, one part skeptical and one part hopeful. If Jericho truly did have a Patron now, a deity who cared, what might that mean for the residents? How might it change them for the better? Loki disappeared, as Viktor checked in with Jupiter. The Magister had grim news for them. Neither the Magisters' Commander or his second had checked in. No one had seen them in several hours. That left Viktor to take over command, at least temporarily. He told Jupiter to relay the message that Argosian ships would be arriving with aid and that the Magisters and Crows should do what they could to assure that the soldiers weren't attacked.

After a short time, heavy-cruisers from the *Kraken* and *Tengu* descended upon the city. True to Mercurius' word, the ships did not attack. Those that could, landed at available paddocks. Those that could not flew into the city and hovered long enough to discharge their cargo of soldiers and supplies.

The soldiers joined with the Crows and mercenaries of Jericho and worked to reestablish control. Several of Mercurius' Technomancers, along with their own contingent of technosoldiers, joined with the Magisters and Artificers of the city to begin rebuilding what had been lost. Within the hour, the pandemonium had died down, the fires raging in the city put out and the citizenry organized to begin sifting through the wreckage and rubble of the city.

Argoth, 10000 ft above the Aryth Ocean, Year of the Jade Bull, 2114 CE

Cadi groaned and cracked her eyes open. She blinked muzzily, trying to figure out where she was. The room was dim and through the curtains of a small window moonlight glowed. She sat up with a sharp cry as she recalled the battle with the minotaur, the riots, the Argosian ships ready to fire, the city's buildings crumbling, crashing down around her and her companions. Just as quickly fell back against the pillow, nausea roiling in her stomach. The noise attracted attention and an Argosian wearing the grey robes of a Technomancer walked in. He murmured something and soft light erupted from an Artifice lamp.

"Well then, so you're finally awake, you are," he said in a cheerful manner. "'Bout time, it is. My name is Sovarius. Let's see how you're doing." He offered a hand and Cadi took it, wincing at the weakness that shook her hands and she frowned at the awkward heaviness of her left hand. Cadi lay quietly as the Technomancer assessed her condition.

"Good, good." He let go of her hand. "Now, lift your left arm for me." Cadi mutely obeyed, frowning again at the puzzling heaviness.

"Good. Touch your fingers to your thumb, one by one, please." Once more Cadi obeyed. Her fingers felt stiff and odd and moved clumsily, but the Technomancer seemed pleased. Sovarius flipped the edge of the blanket back, baring her right leg.

"Very good. Now move your leg for me."

Cadi did so and became more alarmed by the fact that her leg seemed to have the same heaviness as her arm.

"Good. Curl your toes in, then splay them out."

"What happened? Where am I?" Cadi asked as she followed these latest instructions. She winced at the raspy sluggishness of her voice and wondered just how long she'd been out.

"You were in an accident. You'd lost your arm and leg when you came to us. Master Mercurius himself brought you here, to Trinity. You've been out for a few days," Sovarius replied. Cadi took a moment to digest this information.

"I am on Argoth?" she asked quietly. The only 'Trinity' she could think of was the top Technomancer laboratory on Argoth. After a moment, the full import of his statement settled in. "Wait… *who* brought me here?"

Sovarius chuckled. "You are indeed on Argoth, Lady Cadi. Our Patron brought you here to be tended as a favor to Lord Loki." More mirth shook the Technomancer, lighting up his pale brown eyes. "Your Patron is quite protective of you, milady. He's been here often, the past few days.

"It's rather amazing, actually. Thanks to you, Jericho has a Patron. First time for everything, I s'ppose."

Cadi blinked. "Jericho has a Patron?" she asked, thoroughly confused.

"Kas, your guardian claimed your city. Quite impressive actually, so I've heard. A giant fire serpent challenged our ships."

"The serpent was… Loki?" Cadi remembered the wall of fire that had sprung up along the Rim Wall, the roars of the massive flame-crafted drake that had set the city to shivering and its buildings to crumbling. But if… if he had claimed her city and kept the Argosians from destroying it, then the damage was worth it. A few dead versus the thousands that called Jericho home.

"Kas," Sovarius said again. "He made an agreement with our Patron. A treaty if you will."

Cadi lifted her hand, staring at it. Prosthetics. No wonder the limbs felt odd and heavy. Sadness washed over her briefly, passing almost as quickly as it had come. She was alive and mostly whole. There was that to be thankful for.

"Thank you, Master Sovarius, for taking care of me," she said softly. It was rare, Cadi knew, for outsiders to be allowed into Trinity.

"It has been our pleasure, Lady," the Technomancer said with a slight smile. "And speaking of, there is one here most anxious to see you. He will be delighted you are finally awake. Do you feel up to some company?"

Cadi nodded, wondering who it could be. Not Loki, certainly. The Great One would not need to 'wait' for anything. As she thought of him, she felt Wildfire's warm amusement in her mind and a curious satisfaction.

"Very well. I'll send him in." Sovarius departed, the door hissing softly shut behind him. Cadi dozed fitfully, waking once more at a soft knock on her door. The door opened and Viktor was there. The Dashmari started to come through, relief etched on his face, but pulled up short before he was more than a few steps in. Despair flashed across his features and his ears flicked back in a gesture of confusion. Emotions chased themselves across his face and he spun to leave without as much as a single word.

"Viktor, wait," she called out to him in a puzzled tone. "Please don't leave." The Dashmari froze, his body tense, but he didn't turn back around.

"It's good to see you are well, Cadi. I'm sorry… I can't… I can't stay. That would be a bad idea," he said. His voice was soft and he spoke as if he were having trouble with the words.

"Viktor, please turn around. What's wrong? Are you okay?" Cadi asked, struggling to sit up. Viktor hesitated for a moment, before turning around.

"Please… let me go. This can't end well..," he said in the same soft voice. He looked truly desperate now, as if he wanted nothing more than to flee, though she'd never seen the wolf afraid of anything. Cadi's eyes widened slightly as she caught the *other* look in his eyes, a deep and complete hunger and yearning. Pieces fell into place as realization struck the muddled Magister. All the times that Viktor had arranged to be assigned elsewhere, at least once a month. His careful and complete avoidance of her for several days at a time. Rolf's words came back to her, of a lesson on Dashmari culture when she'd asked him why he never seemed interested in the many young women who flocked around him.

"*I am not interested. A Dashmari can tell their true potential mates by scent alone. To us, each person smells unique. For instance, to me, you smell of* kapri. *A potential mate will carry another scent, equally unique. We are… driven to choose and when we do, the others lose that extra scent. We take our mates until death takes one and then things start over again. We don't need to choose, so long as we avoid those possible mates when the scent is strongest.*" He'd gotten quite flustered by this point and ended the conversation with a "*No one here has that for me.*" Cadi had been amused at his sheepishness, but had never brought the subject up with either Dashmari again.

"How long?" she asked softly, though she had a feeling she already knew. Viktor jerked as if she'd slapped him and then his whole frame sagged as if he were suddenly exhausted.

"From the moment we met…" he whispered. "You smell of *kapri* and… you smell of boysenberry."

"But why have you never said anything?"

"The Dashmari way is not your way. You cannot sense these things. I've managed okay until now. Cadi, please… let me go. I promise… you'll never see me again."

"You're just going to leave? Just like that?" Cadi's mind was already reeling from her first realization, but this news cleared her mind.

"I must. I've… stayed too long here now as it is…" he said in a defeated tone, yet he remained still, apparently awaiting her dismissal. This Cadi was reluctant to give. She valued Viktor as a friend and she didn't want to lose that. She tried to regard him in this new light. The Dashmari was several years older than she, but the difference wasn't alarming. He was a handsome man in a rugged sort of way, despite (or perhaps *because of*) the scars that whitened his ears and laced his craggy face.

"Would you have spoken sooner if I had been Dashmari?"

"If you had been Dashmari I would not have needed to say anything," Viktor replied.

"Have you not said anything because I am *not* Dashmari?" Cadi asked. Recalling his protectiveness towards her, Cadi was pretty sure of the answer.

"That has nothing to do with it. I didn't want to make you uncomfortable. Please… *let me go*," he said in a stricken tone.

"Viktor, come here, please," Cadi said, in a voice already growing drowsy from the effort. He shook his head, took a step back, then another and Cadi knew if he made it to the door, if he made it out, she'd really never see him again. She repeated the request and he stopped, ears twitching with uncertainty. She repeated it a third time, holding out her hand. It was enough to propel him forward and the wolf crossed the room in two great strides. Bending over the bed, he caught Cadi's face between his hands and kissed her deeply but gently. When he drew away, she could see tension was gone from him. Uncertainty still lit his eyes and the yearning was still there, though muted somewhat now and she realized that her unspoken acceptance had quelled the larger part of his need, that the touch, the contact, had done this.

"Are you sure of this?" he asked softly.

"I am sure that my life would be much poorer without you in it, Viktor. Of that I am very certain, so yes, I am sure," Cadi replied. She watched the rest of the uncertainty drain from his face with some relief.

Skycity of Port Jericho, 10000 ft above the Aryth Ocean, Year of the Jade Bull, 2114 CE

Four weeks had passed since Loki had claimed Port Jericho as his own and three since Cadi had returned home. The city had been cleaned up and repaired. Little evidence remained of the riots beforehand. Little evidence save for the massive serpent that now ringed the city. The Jerachi citizens looked upon the serpent with a source of pride. No longer were they an unclaimed city. They had a Patron now and they knew it. A Patron who did *not* mind that they were a city of misfits, but rather seemed glad of this fact. Already this was making a difference in how they regarded themselves and how they interacted with the Argosian soldiers still present in the city.

Cadi sighed. And now, everyone knew that *she* was tied to this new Patron and she found herself in the unenviable position of leader of Jericho, given that the previous Lord Governor had perished in the disaster that had struck the city and Lord Loki himself seemed happy to encourage this notion. The Magister missed her former job. It had been simple compared to this. Process a scene. Catch a criminal. Easy enough. Though now, there seemed to be far less crime within the city. Far less saddening work for the Magisters.

With Lord Loki's guidance… Cadi found she could no longer think of him as merely a companion and friend, though he remained such and the bond between them remained unbroken…

things had slowly improved through the whole city. The way Jericho functioned was redefined. In the years to come, though Cadi could not know that now, Port Jericho, once derogatorily called 'Sin City', would earn the name 'Serpent City' and be one of the safest places to live despite the criminal element.

More weeks passed and the Argosians eventually left, but not without securing a formal treaty with Port Jericho, leader to leader, part of which involved a negotiation for trade of the invaluable new mage-metal. By unspoken consent, Cadi had earned the title and position of Lady of Jericho and though the job chafed at her at times, things were improving.

Cadi owed keeping her sanity to Viktor's presence in her life. The Dashmari, now free from the having to hide his feelings, had become an even stronger source of strength. The two of them, along with Rolf, had moved to the Governor's Palace. Cadi had moved there only reluctantly, but the citizens had been insistent.

The Governor's palace had been located in the exact middle of Jericho, nestled within the depths of the largest forested area in the skycity, a hub surrounded by the four Wards. Where before it had just been her, here Cadi found herself surrounded by a plethora of servants, always wanting to 'do' things for her. There were times when she missed her small house in East Ward and the blessed solitude of being a simple Magister.

Much of Thorndagger Manor itself, as the Governor's palace was called, had been destroyed during the disaster and it had been with the assistance of the Technomancers and Artificers that it had been rebuilt as swiftly as it had. The building itself was fairly large and consisted of an inner keep with four tall towers. There was a courtyard encircled by an outer keep with four shorter towers. Lord Loki had claimed one of the innermost towers. That tower was jet black, changed from grey stone to shimmery obsidian by the deity that had made it his own.

That particular tower had no access, save when Loki wished it. The entire complex had a broad yard ringed by the forest itself. Guardian statues now flanked the two paths to Thorndagger, one of each pair facing outward and one inward. Each statue, Loki told her later, was a trickster deity. Cadi recognized one as Loki himself, covered with the raven cloak. Ekkituu, a creature that looked half cat and half dog, guarded the path with the raven man. At the opposite path, another canine, whom Loki had called 'Coyote', shared guard duty with a second feather cloaked man sporting an eagle head, whom Cadi recognized as a representation of Mercurius Greyeyes, the Technomancer Patron.

A small staff of servants lived here along with a tiny contingent of Crows that served as personal guards for Jericho's leader. Thorndagger had also been home to the Governor's adviser, but he had perished during the riots, as had the Governor. Cadi had named Viktor as adviser in his place.

"Torbit for your thoughts?'

Cadi looked up from the paperwork scattered over her desk and smiled as Viktor walked over. He bent to give her a kiss before turning his attention to the paperwork.

"Ah. Export reports. Always fun on a beautiful afternoon."

Cadi glanced out the window, where the sun shone brightly and made a face. She gestured to the pile of papers.

"Well, be my guest. If it sounds so fun, *you* stay here and go through them. I'll go enjoy the sunshine," Cadi muttered. Viktor chuckled and held out a pin. Cadi recognized the dragon and spiral insignia of Drakkengaard and felt a brief sorrow as her thoughts turned to Draccus and the sacrifice he had made.

"No, thanks. I came to tell you I received a message from Dracos. He'd like to see us, the sooner, the better," Viktor said. Cadi was surprised. They hadn't seen nor heard from Dracos since that terrible night and Cadi hadn't been able to bring herself to travel back to the Wyvern's Roost. She stood, stretching hugely.

"Now seems like a good time. If I sit here much longer, I'm going to slowly lose my mind to the sheer boredom of reading these reports."

Viktor chuckled again and matched Cadi's pace as she set off through the keep. Cadi took the opportunity to walk, enjoying the fresh air and the chance to stretch her legs. Paperwork kept her inside much of the time. If she'd thought the paperwork a Magister had to deal with was overwhelming at times, it was a short flight on a clear day compared to the amount the Governor's office handled in a day. Viktor had suggested more than once that she hire people to serve as administrators, but she hadn't done so yet.

Cadi could hear the excited whispers they left in their wake. The Jerachi had come to love their Lady, as much as they revered their new Patron. Anytime she went out now, her presence caused a different kind of stir than she had when she'd been a Magister. A leisurely walk brought them to North Ward and Shadowylde Lane. Nitka greeted them when they entered the Wyvern's Roost. The Arkaddian hunter guided them to the same storeroom they'd visited before. A brief exchange in Argosian and the door to Drakkengaard hissed open. Nitka gestured them through.

"What, you don't want our weapons this time?" Cadi asked. Nitka grinned and shook his head.

"For you, Lady, no. We would not be the ones to offer you insult or offense. You are the Lady of Jericho now. No place is closed to you."

Cadi blew out a huff. The preferential treatment was beginning to get on her nerves. No one wanted to offend Cadi, lest they offend Lord Loki.

"Anywhere, huh? And did the previous Lord Governor have the same privilege?" Cadi asked. She was rewarded with a sheepish look from the hunter. "I thought not. Why am I any different than any other leader Jericho has ever had?"

"Uh… do I really need to answer that, Lady?" Nitka asked. Cadi scowled at him and took the lead through the door, following the corridor to the same common room where they had first met Draccus. Cadi felt the unbidden tears welling up again and she took a slow breath, trying to compose herself. Viktor put a hand on her shoulder, giving a gentle squeeze.

"I know," he said. "The hunter did a brave thing."

"I wish there was some way to repay that," Cadi said, as she walked through the door.

"Matter of fact, there just might be," came another voice and Cadi turned to find Dracos standing where Draccus had once stood. Cadi couldn't imagine how he must feel, to have lost a brother.

"I'm sorry for your loss, Dracos," she said. "Whatever we can do, just ask."

"Very well. Follow me. There's someone as wants to meet you." They followed the Argosian exited the room through a door in the far corner. They walked down a richly decorated hallway, hung with woven tapestries of dragons and the dragon-kin, from wurms to reavers. Dracos stopped and rapped on a door. A muffled voice called out 'Enter'. Dracos touched a panel and the door hissed open.

The room beyond the door was large, but stuffed with all manner of knick-knacks. Two saurian skeletons guarded the entrance and from the ceiling hung the skeleton of a juvenile dragon, its wings brushing the far walls. Bookcases lined with both books and oddities lined most of the available wallspace. A window looked out onto the yawning abyss beyond the Rim Wall. A desk sat before the window and at that desk sat another Argosian, head bent to his work. He finished what he was doing and looked up. Cadi gasped as she found herself staring into the golden eyes of the man she'd seen die in the Labyrinth chamber.

"Draccus!"

The hunter grinned broadly. "None other."

"But... but how. We saw Kellin... You died," Cadi sputtered. Viktor stirred behind her.

"It wasn't you, was it?" he rumbled. "It was a *shaendae*."

"It was and it wasn't," Draccus said. "*Shaendae* is a Dashmari word. It doesn't quite cover the extent of what I did."

"What did you do?" Cadi asked. "What's a *shaendae*?"

"A *shaendae* is something a Dashhuygin can create, a mirror self. It looks like them, acts like them, but... it has no soul," Viktor said.

"*Yethe*, the *shaendae* have no souls, nothing to sacrifice. The person who died was me. A magick unique to the Technomancers, to the *Old Ones* specifically, is the ability to calve the soul. A fragment is a mirror of the whole. I created a subtype of myself, down to every last nuance of my essence. He was me and, if he were still alive, could be reintegrated into my own essence, provided it were done within two weeks of the calving. After that, the subtype becomes their own being, an identical twin of sorts."

"You... created a being, only to sacrifice him?" Cadi asked slowly, thinking of the cheeky man whose final request had been a kiss. "What if he didn't want to die? You created a new life. Doesn't that mean anything?"

"It was necessary," Draccus said. "A preservation of our knowledge and the ability to fulfill the sacrifice so that the beast could be contained, but... if it makes a difference to you... it was the primary who completed the sacrifice. It is the essence that retains memories and an Old One can change bodies at will, by transferring the soul chip. This is little different and I am still Draccus. It was I and not Dracos who was there that night. I watched myself die. Not something pleasant, but you gave him a parting gift quite unexpected."

"But… doesn't getting rid of part of your essence cause problems?" Cadi asked.

"Sometimes," Draccus acknowledged. "Sometimes it is enough to cause the new body to fritz, a danger I'd already survived when I underwent Conversion to begin with. The calving, perhaps, left me a little more insane that I already was. I don't know. I can't tell."

"I thought those who fritzed were… put down?" Viktor asked.

"They are, as I should have been. I slew the Architects who had performed the Conversion and those who tried to stop me. I fled and found a way to put the compulsions I now felt to a more… constructive… use. My Patron has guided me these many long years, helping me to master control. I came here, to Jericho, and founded one of the better hunter's guilds this city has."

"Is… Dracos a subtype too?"

"*Yethe*. Dracos is my *al'raj*, though he is more like my brother."

Cadi nodded. She knew what an *al'raj* was. They were beings the Technomancers created, with bodies like those of the Old Ones and personality traits and characteristics devoid of essence, which Cadi now understood to be soul essence, distilled from volunteers. The vital spark of soul essence was provided by Mercurius himself, through a conduit. The *al'raj*, or *al'raja* for females, usually tended the Technomancer labs, ships and other facilities.

"I'm glad to… know the truth, but why did you call us here? What could we possibly do for you?" Cadi asked.

"Not for me. For the one who gave his life, for both of them. I did want to let you know the truth. I also wanted to express my thanks, for you brought a Patron to us." Draccus looked down at the desk and pushed a tech-slate over to her. On it was a detailed drawing of the minotaur towering over the fallen form of a winged man and a defiant man in a miner's lamp. "And I want permission to erect a statue like this in the East Ward plaza. They deserve it."

Cadi nodded. "Certainly. I can arrange for some of the Artificers to help you."

"No need. I'd prefer to do it alone. But... I'd like to request some of the *tryllym* to create it. A pallet of ingots the Artificers have crafted should serve nicely. Just name your price."

"No price. Where do you want it delivered?"

Draccus frowned at her offer. "It's too valuable to give away. As for where, just have them move it to the front of the storage vault. I can get it from there and it's much closer to the plaza."

"Done. It'll be there tonight. And I'm not giving it away. That price has already been paid, by both of them."

At her words, Draccus' face grew solemn. "So it has. *Dos mere,* Lady Cadi. If ever you have need of us, or just wish to visit, do stop by. Drakkengaard is always open to you."

Cadi and Viktor made their farewells, returning to Thorndagger via the East Ward mining vaults. The Artificers there had given her odd looks, but hadn't argued about the strange order to move a pallet of the *tryllym* ingots to the front of the storage vault. And in the morning, Cadi was hardly surprised when servants woke her and Viktor with the news that a *tryllym* statue had appeared in the East Ward plaza overnight, with no evidence as to how it had gotten there and she smiled at the thought of the stealthy drakeen hunter jumping the mage-metal out of the vault and crafting a statue with it under the noses of the Crows and Magisters patrolling the Ward.

Lightning Source UK Ltd.
Milton Keynes UK
UKHW021843110321
380204UK00010B/578/J